Totally Bound Publishing books by Aliyah Burke:

Through the Fire
Seducing Damian

Code of Honour
A Marriage of Convenience
The Lieutenant's Ex-Wife
A Man Like No Other
When Stars Collide

In Aeternum
Casanova in Training
Harbour of Refuge
Protected by Shadows

Interludes
Temporary Home

I0542082

Interludes

ALONE WITH YOU

ALIYAH BURKE

ALONE WITH YOU

Dedication

To all my readers, thank you from the bottom of my heart for your amazing support.
To my husband, I don't know how it is possible but I love you more every day.
And as always, to the men and women who serve this country, thank you for your selflessness, sacrifice and all you do to keep us safe. To you and your families, I thank you!

Chapter One

Ariel Greene trudged up the steps to her fourth floor apartment after completing her early morning run. Fighting off a yawn, she dug for her key and unlocked the door. Once she'd showered and dressed in shorts and tank top, she went to her coffeemaker gratefully looking forward to that first cup.

There was none. No hot java brew set to make her a nice person and capable of facing her day.

"What? I thought I pre-programmed it." The moment she opened the filter's cover, she knew why the pot sat empty. Someone had forgotten to buy coffee upon their return. "Good job, Greene." Sure, it had been late when her plane landed, but to forget to swing by a twenty-four hour store and pick some up...egregious error on her part.

After swiping her favorite mug off the counter, she headed for the door. Six-thirty in the morning. If one was to be awake, coffee—and never any of the decaffeinated type, which in her eyes was sinful and disgraceful—was a must.

Across the hall, she turned the knob and let herself into the apartment. The thick, aromatic scent of coffee greeted her like a familiar friend and she nearly groaned in orgasmic pleasure.

The man behind the island — who'd glanced up as she entered — gave her a smile. "Morning, Ariel."

"Hey, Steve." She hefted her cup, brushed some hair back from her eyes and yawned for what seemed to be the umpteenth time in two minutes. "Need coffee."

He tucked some blond hair behind his left ear. "Help yourself. I thought you might be by."

Steve Yost was a lean man. Sweet as the dickens and totally not her sexual type. Which was a pity, for she could use a friend with benefits — one who lived across the hall, even better. He was, however, a great neighbor and friend. His roommate, on the other hand, had her panties wet just by walking in the room.

She fixed her coffee then propped a hip against the platform where Steve worked and blessedly took that first life-giving drink. Hot or not, she couldn't function without this stuff. "How have you been?"

"Busy. Good, though. You?"

"Obviously not well enough to remember to bring coffee home after a trip so I have some in the apartment."

He smiled, a flash of straight white teeth against tanned skin. "How was Seattle?"

"Damn sight cooler than here, for one." She drank some more java and purred in contentment. Things were aligning right in her world. Today *could* be a good day now that she'd had some caffeine.

"And the wedding?"

She flexed her fingers about the mug. "Absolutely perfect. Roxi made such a beautiful bride." A grin. "Sam was pretty hot as well. So were the rest of the

Marines standing up with him. And the ones in the audience."

Her friend, Roxi Mammon—now Roxi Hoch—had gotten married this past weekend. She and Roxi had served together in the Corps and Sam—her new husband—still did.

"Thanks for getting my mail," she said, falling silent when a leggy blonde strolled into view. One eyebrow rose and she knew exactly what room that woman had come from.

"This your girlfriend, Steve?" The question was asked with a thick Texas drawl.

"Nope. Our neighbor."

"Oh." Her smile came sugar-sweet. "I'm Daisy. Spent the night with Tuck."

Daisy? Of course you are. "Congratulations?" Ariel did her best to keep her emotions subdued. Hard to do when she longed to punch her in the nose. *I have no reason to be jealous. It's not like he's mine or anything.*

Before little Ms Daisy could say another word, the man himself ambled around the corner. Tuck Carter. Construction worker. Hot as sin. Not to mention the star player in many personal fantasies that had her reaching for the drawer that held a few toys.

Bronzed skin, jet black hair and brown eyes that could turn her to mush. He wore jeans—currently unbuttoned—that formed tight to his body, and nothing else. A smile split his bow-shaped lips when he spied her.

"Ariel. You're back." He poured himself some coffee and sat on a counter. "How was your trip?"

"Great. Looks like you're having fun."

His grin was intoxicating as usual and her panties dampened. Also, as usual.

"You know me."

"Not as well as some in this room," she tossed out casually.

"You have people just walk into your apartment?" Daisy asked, sidling up to Tuck and leaning against him, as if trying to put her claim on him.

"Ariel's not just anyone, she's our neighbor and yes, she does," Tuck said without looking away from Ariel. "Jealous, Ariel?"

Hell yeah! She stood upright, lifted her mug and toasted him. "You wish." Attention on Steve, she gave him a smile. "Thanks for the elixir, hon. You saved my day. Catch ya later."

Then she walked out and back across the hall to her apartment where she sat on her couch and began opening her mail. The knock on her door wasn't all that unexpected. "It's open," she called out. An act she followed by taking a deep breath.

It was a good thing too, for in stepped Tuck. Still clad in only jeans, he filled her doorway with the width of his shoulders.

"You okay?" He sauntered in the apartment. In doing so, her pulse and core temperature skyrocketed.

"Why wouldn't I be? Got what I needed." She lifted her mug to show him.

He watched her intently before making himself comfortable on the love seat across from her. Lord, the man had muscles on muscles. A six pack was his abdomen and she had fantasies—numerous—about licking them. Licking stuff off them, trailing her tongue over the dips and swells.

His thighs, encased as they were in those jeans, were powerful and drool-worthy. *If I don't want to make a fool of myself, I better not keep this up.*

Closing her eyes, she took another deep breath. He hadn't moved and she was okay with that. Art, after all, should be appreciated. And the man before her—a masterpiece.

"Just checking. You making breakfast?"

"Sure. You covered the coffee." She placed the stack of mail on the end table. "I ain't feedin' your…overnight guest, though."

His deep laughter rolled from his gut and he pushed to his feet. "Babe, you're *all* the woman I need. I'm just waiting on you to give me the green light." He leaned close, bringing along the rugged masculine smell that always surrounded him. That panty-soaking, pulse-accelerating scent.

Lord help her, those lips were right there. "Isn't that what the blonde did?"

"A few times. Wanna hear deets?"

Not even if hell froze over. "Wow, although oh so tempting," she drolled, "I don't need your adventures. I'm a big girl. I've had my own. Thanks, though."

His gaze narrowed slightly as her cell rang.

She smiled at the name on the screen. "'Sup, Helter Skelter? Give me a sec, okay?" Turning the phone slightly, she focused back on a now scowling Tuck. "Tell Steve thirty minutes. Thanks."

"How are you?" she asked into the phone. "I just left you a few hours ago." She walked to the kitchen. "Surely you couldn't miss me already."

Her apartment door slammed a bit harder than necessary and she grinned. Josh 'Helter Skelter' Jones was a Recon Marine who served with Sam and the two of them had hit it off right away. She talked to him the entire time she made breakfast, ending the call when a sharp knock preceded Tuck and Steve's entrance.

"Perfect timing."

Unfortunately, Tuck had put on a shirt. He remained quiet through the meal, which worked. His voice did *things* to her, so it was just as well he didn't participate much in the conversation.

Steve left shortly after he finished, having to get to work. Tuck remained. He sat on the arm of her couch and braced against the back.

"Who's this Helter Skelter?"

She wiped down the table. "Marine who was at the wedding."

"And you gave him your number?"

She paused and stared at him "Why the interest?" *Hope he can't see the jig I'm dancing on the inside.*

"Just trying to look out for you."

"Thanks, but I'm fine."

Tuck grunted and began playing toss with one of her throw pillows from the couch.

"How long have we known each other?"

"Going on two years, why?" He stopped and looked at her.

"Just wondering if I'd needed looking after in that time?"

"No."

She raised an eyebrow in his direction. "Okay then."

He made another noise, very similar to a grunt. "Point taken." He stood. "I'm off to work as well. See you later."

"See ya." She watched him leave and when the door shut behind him, she lowered her head. "God. He's hell on my libido."

She gave herself a few before she got back to cleaning. Tuck... She shook her head. *Nope, it's not a good idea. It's just not.*

Ariel had just finished when the door popped back open and Tuck's dark head ducked in again.

"I forgot." He pointed at her. "Got us tickets to the baseball game. You in?"

"Absolutely!" She loved baseball. "What time?"

"Let's leave about five. That way we can watch some of the pre-game stuff."

"I'll be ready."

His wink sent tremors through her. "See you then."

And just like that, he was gone.

"I should really spend the day in bed with my vibrator just so I can have the edge taken off." She chuckled. If only. If *only* that would work.

* * * *

Pierce 'Tuck' Carter watched his friend and neighbor from his periphery as they rode the bus to the game at Nelson Wolff Stadium. It wasn't uncommon for them to ride on VIA Metropolitan Transit—they didn't have to worry about parking or drinking at the game that way. While there wasn't a major league baseball team in their city, they enjoyed watching the San Antonio Missions, a minor league team.

Ariel had her dark brown hair in a ponytail and drawn through the back of her baseball cap—a Missions hat. She also proudly displayed a black Missions shirt. Her long, toned legs poured out from a cock-hardening pair of light gray shorts.

He'd had fantasies about those legs. Wet dreams, which ended in him needing to wash his sheets. He longed to have her legs wrapped around him. Waist. Neck. Ears. All. Any.

The rest of her was to die for as well. Ariel was fit and active, something he liked. He wasn't the sort who stayed inside a lot. He preferred to be outdoors.

A scowl crossed his face at the thought of that call she'd gotten earlier in her apartment. That look of joy on her face had been like a dagger to his heart. Then he'd grown pissed.

No man should make her smile like that.

"What's wrong?" she asked, nudging him with her shoulder. "Were you supposed to be with blondie tonight?"

She says it so casually, as if it doesn't bother her in the least. He shook his head and glanced at her. Her eyes sparkled with trouble and he nearly leaned in and kissed her.

"No way."

"One you needed to have get lost, ASAP?"

"Clingy," he admitted. "Was talking about our next date even before she rolled out of my bed."

"Shouldn't bring them home. Supposed to go to their place."

He took her hand and stared at the back of it. Her skin was smooth and supple. Spinning her black tungsten band with the laser engraved Celtic design that graced her index finger, he asked, "Is that what you do?"

"Pretty much," she replied easily.

He didn't like her response but he was glad she didn't pull away from his touch. She wore a few rings like that, all black bands with designs on them. Both hands, some on her thumbs.

"You know, you could always tell them it was time to leave if you have a problem with that whole cuddling thing after."

"Don't you think that would be rude?"

"No worse than you avoiding their calls and trying to pretend you don't see them when you meet out in public a few weeks later. Not to mention trying to get them out of your apartment in the morning. Daisy seemed pretty content there." She took her hand back.

He smirked at the way she drew out Daisy's name. Leaning close, he inhaled her scent. Lilacs. That's what she smelled of. Like when a huge bunch of lilac trees and bushes are in full bloom and the scent is in the air, surrounding you and teasing your senses.

"See, it's comments like that which have me thinking you're jealous."

Her laugh was light and cheerful. "Good thing you're not arrogant or anything."

He rolled his eyes and dropped his arm around her shoulder, glaring at the two men sitting across from them who stared at her.

"You'd know, babe," he said louder, so his words would reach those two. "You know I am well deserving of my arrogance — at least that's what you scream at night."

She rested her head against his shoulder. "All that and more, sweetie. All that and more."

His cock snapped to attention as she pressed her lithe body into him. Lord, he was ready to take her right there. To hell with that law about doing such things in public view. The bus slowed and he stood before helping her to her feet.

Ariel was still laughing as they got off the bus. "I'm beginning to think you just like scaring some men."

There was no need to comment. She had it right. He couldn't explain why he felt possessive when it came to her. It's how it was. Not that it appeared to bother her for the most part.

He stared down at the top of her head. She reached his shoulder and he knew she would be perfect against him in bed. Steve had told him repeatedly not to ruin the easy relationship they had with her as a neighbor. At first he'd thought Steve had been interested in her in a sexual way, but his roommate had assured him that wasn't the case. He just liked her and didn't want there to be tension when it got messed up.

After producing the tickets at the gate, they walked in and headed for their seats. The ballpark was mostly empty, part of why they'd come so early. They both enjoyed watching batting practice.

"Nice seats," she said as she slipped into hers.

"Got them from a client who said he couldn't make the game."

"How's the construction biz going? Or coming, rather?"

"We're staying busy so it's nice. I think we're about to get another client—boss was saying it was something big. Who knows." He propped his feet up on the back of the chair before him. "How about you? Work going okay?"

That was the one thing they didn't talk much about. She was fairly tight-lipped on what she did—he knew she dealt with security but that was it. Only recently had she taken to letting them in her apartment with just an 'It's open.' Took her a while to just walk into their place as well. But they'd been neighbors for nearly two years now and looked after each other. Wasn't that difficult, they occupied the only two apartments on their floor.

"Keeps me hopping. I'm sure I'll have a lot to catch up on tomorrow. But I refused to miss Roxi's wedding."

That comment reminded him again of the man who'd called her. "Right, the Marine."

"The Marine? Who...oh, are you talking about Helter Skelter? Yes, Recon Marine to be exact." She grinned and waggled her eyebrows.

He grunted and shook his head. "I need a beer, want anything?"

"Beer and nachos."

Tuck got to his feet and walked off. Sure, it was great she didn't mind eating in front of him, he liked that. But he despised the light in her expression when she spoke about Marines.

He got some food for them and their drinks. She was sitting there, head bobbing to the music that played through the stadium as the Missions finished up their BP—batting practice.

"Gonna get up and dance?" he asked with a grin.

"I don't know. I just may." She sat up a bit more and reached for the stuff he handed her. "Thanks."

The game was exciting and close up to the end, when the Missions finally pulled off the 'W' against the Corpus Christi Hooks. He stood alongside Ariel for the final three outs as she cheered on the pitcher to throw strikes. At the final recorded strike, she let out a huge cry and hugged him.

While it had happened previously at other games— it was how she was, she always hugged after a win— he reveled in each time she allowed this type of contact between them.

"Thank you so much for bringing me."

"I can't imagine Steve here."

"No, he prefers his basketball. But at least you have someone to attend Spurs games with."

"You should learn to like the sport."

She snorted and stepped from his arms. "Not likely, so don't hold your breath. Not something I enjoy watching. I'm good for most other sports, though."

"Let's get something to eat."

"Food's on me," she said, gesturing for him to file out with the rest of the fans.

There was an image he could live with. Chocolate sauce, honey, butterscotch. Oh, definitely he could see any of those—or all—dripped all over her body as she lay there waiting for him to lick it off every single inch…

"Great," he managed to choke out.

He maneuvered her in front of him as they exited then went to the bus stop. It was a short ride later before they were seated at a table in a bar and grill. She had a rum and Coke while he had another beer. Chatter was light and flowed easily between them. He truly enjoyed spending time with her—unusual, if he wanted to think about it. Most of the time he hung with men, slept with women. But her, he liked hanging with. *Doesn't stop me from wanting to sleep with her, that's for sure.*

They were on one of the last buses as they made their way back to their apartment. As they entered, he steered her away from the stairs. "Let's take the elevator."

"I always take the stairs," she uttered, her words nearly slurred.

They were both buzzed.

"Not tonight, babe." He pressed the button and they waited for the car to arrive.

Facing him, Ariel licked her lips. "I may not ever have the courage to do this again, Tuck Carter. So I'm going to do it now."

"What's that?" he asked, staring down into her medium brown eyes.

She did it again—licked her full, plump lips—almost distracting him. "I have to tell you something."

The elevator arrived and they got on. He engaged the button for their floor. "What'd you have to tell me, Ariel?"

She waggled her finger in his direction. "You, Tuck Carter."

He grinned at her. "You've already said that bit."

"Oh." Her lips pursed briefly. "Just so's you know, I go through so many batteries because of you, it's not even funny. And just once, I want to know what it's like to kiss you."

Her proclamation stunned him and he stood frozen to the spot. Didn't matter, Ariel was strong and jerked him to her, plastering her lips to his. A rumble rolled up from his chest and all sense flew out of the window as he gathered her up in his arms and intensified the kiss. Her taste, incredible. Her curves against him, sinful.

In the back of his mind, he knew they'd just crossed some kind of line. Right here, right now. He didn't give a damn. All that mattered was she was wrapped around him like a lover, like *she* should be. He'd face the consequences later.

Chapter Two

Ariel stirred slightly when her internal clock went off. Lord, she was sore. There wasn't a part of her body that didn't ache. Not in a bad way but in one she'd not expected.

She could smell him around her. Tuck. The scent of his body and soap filled her nose and she didn't bother opening her eyes. Every morning waking from her dreams of him, the moment she lifted her lids was when reality came crashing back in. She didn't want that.

I feel like I've gone rounds in the sparring ring at Basic. What the heck did I do last night? We went to the game then out to a bar.

Realizing she couldn't ignore her screaming bladder any longer, she cracked open her eyes, unsure if she'd remembered to draw her shades last night before she stumbled to bed. Her breath caught in her throat as she found herself staring at walls, eggshell in hue. The shelves on them held books and a few things she knew weren't in her room.

Alone With You

Panic reached out its arms and gave her a large hug, welcoming her into the fold. Where the hell was she? And what was she doing thinking about Tuck if she'd gone home with someone else? The body behind her shifted and a hard physique rubbed against her. Sparks of longing flitted to life within and she had to clamp down on her lips to keep the moan from slipping free.

Turning slowly, she peered over her shoulder to see whose bed she was in. If she'd thought her previous panic had been bad, seeing Tuck's face right there in slumber kicked it into hyper drive.

Oh my God. Holy fuckin' shit. I'm in bed with Tuck? I'm in bed with Tuck!

He slumbered on, unaware of her dilemma. His thick lashes rested upon his bronzed skin. Was it possible for someone to look better sleeping? She wasn't sure, but he might be able to.

Not what I need to focus on right now. I have to get out of here.

That was it. No more drinking. *Yeah right.* Okay, no more with Tuck in range. She wasn't sure how this had happened but she had to get out before he woke up. Her fantasies of him were one thing but she'd not had plans to make them come to fruition.

Slipping soundlessly from the bed and his warmth that had been around her like... Nope, don't need to go there either. She jumped into her clothes, bypassing the panties and shoving them in her pocket. Shoes in one hand, she cracked open the door to his room and stepped through.

Now, if she could just make it to the door. She tiptoed by Steve's door and out into the living room. It didn't matter. Steve Yost sat there on the sofa, a book in one hand and his coffee in another.

21

"Morning, Ariel," he said in his familiar drawl.

Heat raced up her cheeks and she hoped he couldn't see the redness because her face had to be flaming for sure. She blew a puff of air and shrugged hopelessly. "Don't tell him you saw me, please."

"You know he'll ask."

She shook her head, unable to deal with this right now. In her head, she imagined Tuck was waking up and on his way out to where she *desperately* wanted to leave.

"I just... I can't, Steve." She bolted, making sure not to slam the door.

Back at her apartment, she engaged the locks and slumped against the smooth wood, breath hitching, longing to curl into a small ball. *What the hell did I just do?*

Possibly ruined a great friendship. That sucked—she truly enjoyed both of them. But she'd seen numerous times how he treated women he slept with so casually.

Pushing up from the floor, she stumbled to her bedroom and subsequently into the shower where she took a long one until she could no longer smell his scent, which had embedded itself into her skin and mind. Beneath the pounding spray, she did her best *not* to recollect how it had been in his arms. Unfortunately that was easier said than accomplished. Her memory had returned full force and in doing so, didn't leave a single experience untouched.

Her phone was ringing as she stepped out from the bathroom with a towel about her midsection. Reaching for it, she checked the screen to see who it was before answering.

"Greene."

"Ariel. You back?"

"I'm back, Slater. What's up?"

Slater McKenzie was her boss and had recruited her to come to San Antonio to work for the company there.

"Can you make it in today?"

Could she? Hell yes. Not being home was a great way to avoid someone. "Absolutely. Just let me change" — she looked at her towel and figured he didn't need to know that's all she wore — "and I'll be right in."

"No need to be dressed in business attire. It's a day off so just be comfortable." He hung up.

Comfortable. A word she could agree with. Shucking the towel, she made her way to the dresser where she grabbed everything she would need. It didn't take her long to dress then she shoved her feet into her canvas slip-ons.

She gave her reflection a once-over as she hung the towel back up in the bathroom. Much better than wearing a skirt or pants suit. There were days she missed her uniform from the Marine Corps.

"Well, the cammies. I could do without the skirts." She clicked off the light as she left the room. Purse in hand along with her keys, she peered out of the peephole and shook her head. "What are you going to do, Greene, if you see him there? Head out the window and down the fire escape?"

When she caught herself thinking it could be done, she sighed and left her place. Thankfully, there was no one else around. After locking up, she hastened down the stairs to the ground floor and quickly made her way to her vehicle. Her silver LR3 had been her gift to herself after she'd gotten out of the Corps. Not brand new — she'd bought it pre-owned and certified. Loved it.

Before too long she was on her way, driving through the hushed streets of San Antonio. Showing her badge at the building security gate, she smiled at the man there.

"Morning, Dale."

"Ariel. You're here today?"

"Got called in. You on all day or leaving soon?"

"Just got here myself."

She nodded. He was a happy man who never failed to make her smile. "I'm sure I'll see you later then."

"Yes, ma'am. Have a good one."

The bar lifted and she drove into the covered parking lot. Up on the fifth floor, she parked then got out. Alarming her SUV as she walked toward the elevator bay, which also held the stairs and doors to the building, Ariel couldn't help but think back to waking in his bed. They'd not gotten much sleep and even now after the hot shower, she continued to experience the ache in her muscles.

"Not sure how come I didn't know whose bed I was in the second I woke up." She shrugged off the memories and focused on not looking like a woman who'd just rolled out from beneath her lover before coming in.

Slater was striding through the office when she entered. He raised his coffee mug in her direction as he took a bite of the doughnut he carried. She gave a brief wave in return, immediately feeling a bit self-conscious. Slater wore a suit—granted it was rumpled and stained, but he wasn't in cargo capris and a T-shirt.

"Meeting room. I'll be back in five," the man mumbled before vanishing from view.

Ariel looked around—the place was deserted. She made her way to the meeting room and walked in.

Papers, as well as empty takeout containers, were scattered over the large oak tabletop.

Connie Ling, another woman at the firm, looked up and gave Ariel a tired smile as she entered. "He got a hold of you then? Good to see you. How was the wedding?"

"What the hell is going on here, Connie?" A slight grin. "Good to see you as well. The wedding was wonderful. I'll tell you about it later. Catch me up."

"I'll do that," Slater spoke from behind her. He moved past her to settle himself in the middle of most of the mess.

Ariel made her way to that end of the table then placed her purse down in a chair and sat in one next to it. "I'm all ears."

Slater was a handsome man. A fit black man who had a mere sprinkle of gray at his temples and a gold hoop in one ear. He had tattoos on his arms they rarely got to see, for most of the time he wore a suit.

"We've been asked to do a security plan for the new museum that's being built."

She rocked back in the chair, still unaware as to why he was so stressed. "Okay, that's not uncommon. What's the —" She gestured to the mess before them.

"It's because of how fast they want it. The company they had gone with first" — he took a drink of coffee — "has been accused of some very unsavory and unflattering things. So they're distancing themselves. Anyway, they want us to go there the day after tomorrow and meet one of their builders so we can tell them where to install things."

"So you just got the plans?"

"Yeah. I'm sending you. You can look over what they have planned and get an idea of what to suggest but I know you'll have some other things to add once you're there."

"You're sending me?" She glanced to Connie for verification.

The slender Asian woman nodded and gave her a grin.

"Do they know how long it usually takes to come up with a plan? And for something the size of this?" She lifted one of the blueprints.

"They're desperate. Any delay and the opening will be pushed back. You can do this, Ariel. You have a knack for it."

She was humbled by his confidence in her ability. "I'll get to work on it right away."

"You sure I didn't take you away from anything at home?"

Tuck's image flashed in front of her face. "Nope. Nothing." She blew out a breath. "So who am I meeting?"

"A man named Pierce Carter. At eight in the morning."

Carter. That was Tuck's last name. Shoving that thought into the darkest hole she could locate, she brushed off her hands. "Okay."

* * * *

"Two days!" Tuck swore, slamming his water bottle down on the counter, sloshing some over the side. With a muttered curse, he wiped it up and dried off his hand. "Two fucking days she's not once answered her door or phone."

Steve glanced briefly at him before returning his attention to the magazine he held. The remnants of their takeout dinner sat on the table behind Tuck, who scooped the trash into the bin.

"Nothing to say, Steve?" He washed his hands and faced his friend. He'd expected to hear something previously from the man who'd been frowning at him for the past two days.

"What do you want me to say, Tuck? I asked you repeatedly not to sleep with her and ruin the friendship we all had. You did and now it's like she vanished."

"She kissed me in the elevator. What was I supposed to do?"

"Keep it in your pants," he replied without humor. "Not treat her like the any number of women she's seen you parade through here."

He threw up his hands and stalked out of the room, only to return moments later. "She's a grown woman, Steve. I didn't force her."

"Never said you did, Tuck. Just like if she now never speaks to us again, you have to be okay with that."

Be okay with that? Was the man insane? "Hell no. She's going to talk to us again. She's not running."

Steve put down the magazine and stared at him. "What is it? That you didn't get the chance to dump her first? Is that what has you so bent out of shape?"

With a theatrical groan, Tuck reigned in his frustration and took a seat. "No. I wasn't going to dump her."

"And she would know this how? Because your track record with women is such that it leads to people thinking of your commitment to commitment?"

"I'm a single man, Steve, just because you don't go out doesn't mean I can't."

"Never said that, man. All I'm saying is from her point of view, why should she be treated any different?" He sliced a hand through the air. "And no, I'm sure I'm not gay."

Okay, so maybe that thought had crossed his mind. The man never—and he meant never—went out.

"So how come you understand women so much?"

"More than a gay man can understand women, Tuck. Come out of the Dark Ages. You want to know how I know? Because I fucked up a relationship and am still paying for it."

Tuck arched an eyebrow.

"I'm married. My wife and I are separated."

There was pain in that announcement. "We've been roommates for four years now."

"Been married all that time."

"No divorce?"

"No!" Steve's exclamation was sharp and definite. "She's my wife. I'm not divorcing her."

"Okay. I'm sorry, man."

"Look, this isn't about me and my up-in-the-air marriage. This is about you and Ariel."

"I'm not giving up, man. She's the one."

Steve leaned forward, nodding as if he weren't the least bit surprised. "You've got your work cut out for you."

Tuck's phone rang. "Yes?"

"Need you to don a suit tomorrow, man. We've got a new company taking over the security layout for the building. I want you there with the electrician to make sure it can all be done," Richard Dockett, his boss, said.

"Me?"

"You want to have your own business one day—this is part of it. I'm en route to Maine for a wedding. I can't make it. Do me proud, boy."

"Who am I meeting?"

"A representative from Prometheus Protections. Not sure who they're sending. This is, as I said, very last minute for them to be joining in. You remember what happened with the other company."

"I recall."

"I want you there so we're not having to tear down walls and all that, which would put us behind schedule."

"Got it. I'll be there, when?"

"Tomorrow at eight."

He hung up and relayed the information to Steve who smiled at him.

"Congrats, man, I know you've been looking to move up and get more experience for what you'd have to do with your own company."

"I know. I'm going to see if she's home."

Steve rolled his eyes and went back to his magazine.

Tuck walked across the hall and knocked on her door. Nothing. "Ariel? Are you in there? If you are come talk to me, I'm not going anywhere." Not a peep. "Christ, what'd you do, go stay at a hotel to make sure you didn't have to see me?"

He stomped back to his place and slammed the door behind him. Making a beeline for his room, he didn't say anything to Steve on the way, then just sat on his bed and dropped his head into his hands with a groan of defeat.

His phone rang again and instead of feeling uplifted by seeing Ariel's number there, he saw Daisy's. "Ariel was right and so was Steve. This is getting ridiculous." He hit 'Ignore' and flopped back on his bed. Ariel wasn't getting away that easily. He hadn't lied when he'd told Steve she was the one.

* * * *

Morning came fast and as he fixed his tie he waited by the coffee machine. Steve gave him a thumbs-up as he walked by. "Good luck."

He appreciated the support but he had no plans on fucking this up. Once he had his coffee in his travel mug, he went down to his truck and drove to the construction site.

Waving to the guys who were on their way to do construction work, he got out and went inside. He saw the electrician, Marvin Patterson, and made his way to his side. "Morning, Marv."

"Hey, man. Good to see you here. Richard told me he was sending you."

"Here's hoping the one they send from the new company won't be as annoying as the other one."

"Amen."

The sound of heels clicking along the floor reached them and together they turned. Tuck's breath caught in his throat. *No way.* He blinked a few times but his vision didn't change. Walking toward him—and Marv—was none other than the woman he'd been trying to get in touch with. Ariel Greene. She had her nose in the file she held and hadn't spotted him yet.

"Gentlemen," she said without looking up. "I'm so sorry to be the last one here, I was just looking..." She trailed off when she finally glanced up to see him.

That's right, sweetheart. I've got you now.

She recovered quickly. "Looking to see where we should begin."

Marv said, "Let me go grab something I forgot from my car. I'll be right back."

Yep, that was panic in her gaze but it only lasted a few seconds. He crossed his arms and stared down at her.

"Two days." He was a bit shocked by the venom that coated such simple words.

"What are *you* doing here? I'm supposed to meet Pierce Carter."

"You are." He sketched a bow. "Pierce Carter at your service."

She gave a shake of her head — almost like she was in disbelief — along with a slight grimace. "Of course you are. You never said your first name was Pierce."

That time he heard the slight condemnation in her voice. Like this meeting situation was all his fault.

"I go by Tuck ninety-nine percent of the time. Besides, it's not like you said you worked for Prometheus Protections."

She gave him a nod. "True. I didn't."

From that statement, it was clear she would have had no problem had he never known. Tuck didn't like the feeling roiling around within him. He wanted to shake her, get some of the emotion he knew lay deep within out of her. Hell, he'd experienced much of it the other night.

She wasn't even looking at him. Ariel had put her attention back on the file she had in her clipboard binder combo. Tuck could see her shoring up the walls around her emotions. Not what he wanted. Beyond her, he saw Marv had been paused by another worker. Focusing back on Ariel, Tuck knew his grin was near feral.

"I want you back in my bed."

That did it. Her head snapped up and she pinned him with a dangerous glare. "Do *not* mention that." Her fingers tightened around the pen in her hand.

"Was it bad?" He smirked. "No, I do remember how many times and how loudly you screamed my name."

Her pupils dilated and he didn't miss her sharp intake of breath. Oh yeah, she knew exactly what he recalled because it lingered all over her face. Their entire night together. However, she composed herself within seconds.

"Apparently a mistake," she snapped before spinning on her heel and stalking to another man he'd failed to see arrive.

Tuck groaned. *It wasn't a mistake, Ariel. And it should be happening more and more.* Then he shifted his attention. "What the hell is he doing here?"

Thomas Schaffer had arrived and was trying desperately to make himself useful to Ariel, from what Tuck could see. The man had no real worth in his opinion. His father was to be the curator and the museum was being built with their family money but Thomas himself... A wastrel would be far too kind a word to squander upon him, in Tuck's mind.

As he prepared himself for the snide remarks that always came from Thomas, Tuck allowed himself to take in Ariel's attire. A dark blue power suit that molded to her in ways that should be considered illegal. No, none of it was overtly sexy. In fact it was very professional—a skirt suit she had paired with sensible heels. All he saw, however, was an ad for sex.

Her hair had been gathered up away from her face to rest in a tight bun upon the back of her skull. Nothing about her said softness. Still didn't change the fact that when he looked, he saw the naked woman who'd lain in his bed, skin flushed with pleasure. Marks from his stubble along her body and love bites from him in places the public would never see. Then, her eyes had been soft and welcoming. Now, nothing but business.

He and Marv arrived at the duo at the same time and Thomas frowned when he looked up and saw Tuck. A smarmy smile lifted his lips and Tuck readied himself for the first slanderous comment to arrive.

"Thought you were just one of the workers, Pierce. Shouldn't you be in a hard hat and up there working with the rest of the men?"

Would it be wrong to punch him in the nose? "Richard asked me to step in for him. But don't worry, we all will be in hard hats." He waved for another one. "Wouldn't want you to feel left out."

Thomas sniffed in derision. "Shall we?"

They all donned their hats. Ariel moved her gaze between the three men and readjusted her clipboard. "After you."

He trailed behind them, eyes more oft than not drifting down to the gentle sway of her ass in that skirt. More things for his wet dreams to work with. Marv dropped back to walk beside him as Ariel had the pleasure of being with Thomas as he talked loudly and pointed things out they specifically wanted as far as security went. She jotted things down and maintained the utmost professionalism. It was a whole other side of Ariel he'd never seen before. She was good. Damn good at her job.

When she had questions for him or Marv she would face them and ask, ignoring Thomas' claim he could answer it all.

Back at the front of the building, she paused. "Thank you for your time, Mr Schaffer. Have a great day."

He inched closer to her, like a kid in a candy store who couldn't keep his hands off the treats. "Maybe we could go to lunch together and discuss your plans."

Glacial cold, her gaze smacked into him. "Sorry. I have things to do and last I knew I was to take this to" — she glanced at her papers — "Gerald Schaffer, not Thomas."

Thomas flushed but recovered quickly. "I could be of help. I can push back my tee time."

Marv coughed under his breath and personally, Tuck wanted to lay Thomas out flat.

"Oh no, any questions I have now will be for Mr Carter or Mr Patterson. You showed me what your family wanted, despite me having that information from your father already in my file. I would *hate* for you to miss your tee time."

Thomas' expression told him this man was one who was used to getting what he wanted. Not only that he wasn't happy when he wasn't allowed to. Right now, the man wanted Ariel. *Like I'm going to allow that to happen.*

Thomas' smile tightened. "You understand golf then, wonderful. Do you play? Perhaps we could play some holes sometime."

There was no way to mistake the underlying meaning there. Tuck shook his head slightly at Marv, who took a step forward. Ariel could handle herself, he knew that much. He also knew her opinion of golf. *This isn't going to go well for Thomas.*

Ariel licked her lips and stepped closer to Thomas. "I don't play," she said, her words succinct and straightforward. "And no, I'm not a fan of the game. In fact, I think it's a waste of time and energy, not to mention water." A small grin — more of a baring of teeth, actually — lifted her lips. "While I understand you don't have anything to do during the day, Mr Schaffer, I'm going to have to ask you to excuse me. I still have a job to do. Have fun playing your game."

Thomas got it that time and walked off muttering under his breath. Then Ariel looked at Tuck, however briefly. She passed on to Marv, pulled a card from her binder then handed it to him. Marv gave her one as well.

"I need to take another walk through the building," she said. "Thank you for your assistance, Mr Carter. Mr Patterson."

Tuck let her get a short distance away. "Ms Greene."

She paused and pivoted, showing the flame pin of her company's logo.

"This is an active construction site. You'll need an escort. I'll be right there."

Her expression was priceless.

"That woman looks like she wants to kill you."

With a smile for Marv, he nodded. "She probably does. We're in the middle of a rough patch."

"So you know her then."

Intimately. "See you later, man."

Marv waved him on and he went back to where Ariel waited, her hardhat seated upon her head. It wasn't fair for someone to look so sexy in one. It was blue, light unlike the dark color of her suit.

"Ready?" he asked, pausing next to her.

Her answer was to stride off. He chuckled and followed.

This could prove to be most interesting and fun.

Chapter Three

This is so going to suck.

Ariel bit the inside of her cheek. It was *so* hard to concentrate with him near. Him. Tuck. Pierce. Whatever the fuck he wanted to call himself. All she knew was she had to focus extra hard *not* to notice how well he filled out his dark charcoal suit.

"Ignoring me won't make me go away, babe."

She sucked on her teeth but continued to keep her back to him as she scanned the ceiling. *Eyes on your own paper.* Came in handy during school years, why not now?

"I'm working, Mr Carter."

"Tuck. You seem to forget we're neighbors. Hell, we're a bit more than that now, wouldn't you say?"

His warm breath teased the back of her neck and she ground her jaw, desperately trying not to lean into his strong body. Ice, she could definitely use some ice right about now. As quickly as he'd moved up, he stepped away to stand beside her. Moments later, some men walked by and inclined their heads, a gesture he returned.

"Gonna tell me why you've been ignoring me for the past two days?"

She closed her eyes before pivoting her hips toward him. "Really? You feel the need to do this now? I'm working. You're working."

"Yes, I do. For all everyone else knows, we're talking about the building and what your company will do to it. I want to know. Two days, Ariel. No response at your door, nothing."

"If you must know," she said, staring down at the papers, "I was at work. This just got handed to us and we had a bunch of work to do on it."

"And you don't have phones at work? I mean, your cell. Which I'm pretty sure I called about ten times."

Okay, so that she felt a bit bad about. "Why?"

"Why what?"

"Why does it matter, Tuck? I know how you treat women you take home to your place. Heck, we talked about it earlier that day. I'm ashamed enough, I don't need to be reminded of it every time I look at you."

A low rumble filled her ear and she glanced up to find him standing close, fury lining every inch of his face. "Ashamed?"

Perhaps that wasn't the right choice of word. Still, she didn't back down. Apparently she didn't respond fast enough for he muttered some words she'd not heard since she left the Corps and grabbed her arm before pushing her back into a room with walls and a ceiling—one of the offices to be. He slammed the door behind him, drowning out most of the sound of the workers surrounding them.

"Ashamed?" His voice had risen.

She held his gaze. "Yes. Come on, Tuck. Are you really surprised by that?"

"Fuck yeah. Am I so vile then, you can't imagine sleeping with me once much less the number of times we did it that night?"

She frowned as she watched him furtively. "Oh, check your fucking ego at the door. Just that morning, *that morning*, I saw little Miss Daisy immediately after she left your bed and I was in it less than twenty-four hours later. *That* is what's making me ashamed. I'm not a baby and won't stand here lying about how attracted I've been to you. But my behavior was inexcusable. I left your bed and ran into Steve. I didn't need him to see that."

"I used protection with her."

She held up her hands and shuddered. "I don't want to think of her and you together. I acted like a slut and I know better. This isn't going to work—it's better I just don't hang with you two anymore."

His expression should have warned her. Should have. His features went blank seconds before he exploded. For a large man he sure could move fast. He had her back against the wall with his mouth slanted over hers.

She purred in pleasure as his taste sank back into her. She slipped her free hand inside his suit coat and around his waist, drawing him in closer. No willpower and no strength. She accepted that.

His rumble ran through her, making her panties damp and her nipples tighten behind her shirt. She closed her eyes and moaned with raw need as he slid one hand up beneath her skirt to her panties. Her moan turned to a gasp when he jerked them off with a snap.

"They seem wet—you don't need to wear them. Because I promise you, Ariel, before we're done going back through this place, I'll fuck you at least five times." His words were graveled and rasped along her skin as he spoke against her lips. He shoved two fingers deep inside her and her legs threatened to give out. "You're already soaked."

"Tuck," she whimpered.

In and out he stroked his fingers, pushing her nearer to the edge she'd been missing since she had left his bed.

"No, not yet." He withdrew his fingers, licked them clean and pocketed her panties. Then he helped straighten up her skirt.

Her gaze lasered in on his groin. His thickness pressed against the pants of his suit and she wove slightly toward it, wanting to touch, lick and more. He readjusted himself then went to the door, opening it.

"This room, Ms Greene, is just like the others. There are two more, which have a different layout. Would you like to see them next?"

It took her several tries to get her reply out. "Yes."

Christ, her legs were wobbly. As they walked along the corridor where the offices were, she tried desperately to regain her breath. It wasn't easy—her heart pounded as if she had just finished running. Her lungs struggled to get any air. And beside her, Tuck walked as if he hadn't a care in the world. She could do as he did. Just had to focus on nonsexual things.

He introduced her to several of the workers they passed—nothing sexual in that. Tuck was the consummate professional. "Right in here," he said, gesturing to a corner office.

Her pulse kicked up in anticipation as she entered. When she'd been through here before, her brain had picked up on things but she hadn't registered them all. Now she was beginning to do that so she could figure out the best plan for them.

Tuck stood behind her. "Do you know how sexy hot you are in that hard hat? I think I'll bring one home and take you while you're wearing it."

Flutters in her belly grew more intense. He didn't touch her physically. But his presence and voice were more than enough to put her close to an orgasm. She stared at her clipboard and jotted down something for this room.

"Are you ready?" he asked.

"Yes." Damn, her voice was so thready and faint it was embarrassing.

"Good, the next room is waiting."

"Rude bastard," she muttered under her breath as she followed him. Lord, her body was strung so tight all it would take for her to come would be a single touch. Moisture dampened her thighs and she prayed it wouldn't get much worse. Slater would kill her if she messed this up.

They passed a small room, which was going to be a closet. There was no door and she barely looked at it, knowing already what it would have in it. Tuck wrapped an arm around her waist and lifted her in there. Before she knew what was happening, he slid his thick cock deep inside her with one stroke.

"Ohhh," she moaned. On the other side of the wall she could hear the skill saw running.

"Hands on the wall," he ground out.

She complied as he thrust in and out of her pussy. Contracting her muscles around him, she whimpered as he moved faster.

Tuck held her so the dusty wall wouldn't leave anything on her suit. It also meant she couldn't brace well against his driving cock. He controlled it all and he was making her suffer. Fast then slow. Deep then shallow. She wanted to scream in frustration. Her limbs trembled with the force of her release but he was sending her right back up to the precipice without a break. Not that she wanted one.

"Are you ashamed now?" he asked in an angry tone.

Angry? She could barely think straight. Because of the hard hat she wore, she rested her head on the wall as well. The hand holding the clipboard trembled as she tried to keep it from sliding to the floor and making a mess.

"Fuck me, Tuck," she begged.

"I am. Answer my question."

In and out. Back and forth. Lord, she was going to scream at the top of her lungs in a moment.

"No."

He pressed her tight to him, changing the angle of his strokes. "I can feel you around me, Ariel. So tight and about to come again. Your muscles are gripping me unlike anything I've ever experienced before. I'm not giving this up. I'm not giving up on us."

"Need...to...come."

"Yes, yes you do." He slowed then shoved once more deep inside her. She splintered around him as he growled in her ear before lifting her off him.

Legs shaky, she held onto him as she waited for her stability to come back. Bless the man, he had something to clean up with. Still floating in bliss, she didn't care where he'd gotten the paper towels or why he had them.

They got back on their way and he tossed the used paper towels into the first receptacle they passed. Again, the man looked all kinds of put together. She, on the other hand, felt like everything was out of place. If it was, not a single person glanced at them oddly. The men were all nice and professional to her, treating her with respect.

After coming the third time, she could barely catch her breath. This time he'd taken her face to face, again holding her so she didn't get dirty. And after they'd cleaned up, she stood by the window overlooking a swathe of green grass and tried to make sense of what was happening.

He was turning her inside out.

* * * *

Tuck threaded his fingers along the satin of her panties he still carried in his pocket. The material was cool to the touch—quite the opposite of its former wearer. Hot. That was the only way to explain her. Volcanic. Explosive.

Six times since they'd been left alone in the museum by the others and he wasn't done with her. Not by a long shot. He'd meant those words he'd uttered. At least five times. At least. And he'd managed six. The urge to shoot his load inside her was overwhelming, but he'd refrained.

He refused to let her be ashamed by what they'd shared. Her words had pissed him off no end. Granted some of what she'd said was true, especially that part about Daisy, but he and Ariel were different. Friends. Neighbors.

Now as he stood there on the top of the steps to the museum, he watched her stride away to her Land Rover. It may have been his imagination but he would have sworn she looked a bit shaky on her legs there. He wiped away his masculine smirk when she glanced at him over her shoulder. He might be arrogant but he wasn't stupid enough to provoke a Marine—technically an ex-Marine—who wasn't all too pleased with him. Attracted to? Yes, definitely. Happy with? Nope.

She slammed her driver's door harder than necessary and he gave her a little wave before she drove away. He would stop by and see her tonight. He grinned again. They could pick up where they'd left off today. With him buried deep inside her.

Tuck called Richard and filled him in on how things had gone with Ariel—thankfully he remembered to call her Ms Greene. Then he headed home, since Richard told him to go.

Steve wasn't there when he entered and Tuck went straight to his room and took off the suit, showered then dressed in clothing he preferred to wear. Jeans and a tee. He kept busy until the time he knew Ariel would come back from work. Then he went to the door and opened it, resting in the frame and waiting for her to come around the corner.

"She's not coming home," Steve said as he stepped from the elevator.

"What?" He cleared his throat. "What are you talking about?"

"Ariel, she's not coming back tonight." He shifted the bags he held and Tuck stepped back, allowing him to pass unimpeded.

It took him a moment to formulate a response that wasn't drenched in possessiveness. "How do you know this?"

"Ran into her at Mighties. She was picking up some lunch and told me she wouldn't be joining us for dinner."

A rumble of discontent rose within him. "Okay."

"So, how'd it go today?" Steve began putting away the groceries he'd returned with.

"Good," Tuck said. *Excellent in some parts.* "We're working with Ariel's company."

Steve paused, holding a box of pasta in one hand. "Ariel's company?"

Tuck shut the door behind him and went to help his roommate. "The one she works for. Prometheus Protections."

"And how'd that work with the two of you having fucked loud enough to wake the dead?"

"We were professional. Got the job done and she'll be getting back to me with the things she'll need or any questions." He flipped an apple up a few times before biting into it. "Didn't think she'd be hiding out at her office, though."

Steve glared at him and Tuck held up his hands. "I know, I know. You told me not to mess it up." Tuck shoved a hand through his hair. "It's not like I forced her, Steve," he said, reiterating his defense from earlier.

"We've gone over that, Tuck. All I know is my own neighbor is embarrassed to look me in the eye now because my roommate has fucked her brains out. I liked her. A lot." He folded the bag with a snap then walked away.

Tuck rolled his eyes and reached for his phone. Calling Ariel, he waited for her to pick up. She never did.

"Ariel. You need to call me back. We need to talk."

Five minutes later, his phone rang. "Hello?"

"Is this business related, Mr Carter?" Ariel's tone flowed like smooth melted chocolate from her mouth to his ear.

"You know it's not and would you stop calling me that?"

"I'm sorry then. I have work to do."

In the background he could hear a man's voice and he frowned when she didn't wait for another moment, just hung up. He scowled and with a careful, deliberate action, he set his phone away from him. He wouldn't continue to call her, he wasn't that bad off.

Right.

He went to work in his room on some plans of the house he was designing for himself. It was a labor of love and he worked on it whenever he had some time. What better way for someone to see what he was capable of doing than to be able to say he'd not just built, but also designed his own home.

* * * *

The night was long and he woke to Steve shutting the door in the living room. Sitting up, he wiped a hand down his face then climbed off his bed and walked out to the main area. Steve was dressed and had a pastry in his hand.

"What's going on?" he asked.

"Nothing, just saying good morning to Ariel." Steve sat on the couch.

"She's home?"

"Nope, just left. Came home for a shower and to change. I was on my way back from the bakery when I ran into her."

Tuck went to the door and looked out. Of course she wouldn't still be in sight. Ariel hated taking the elevator. He shut the door with more force than necessary and glared at his roommate who was not paying him any mind.

Showering didn't do much to improve his disposition and as he strode for the door, Steve called to him.

"I'll not be back tonight. Have to make a day trip to Dallas and will be there overnight."

Shoving his own thoughts back, he turned to look at Steve. "Is this dealing with your wife?"

"In a manner of speaking, yes."

"You going to be okay, man?"

Steve's smile was tense and strained. "Maybe someday. Anyway, just wanted you to know."

"Let me know if there's anything I can do."

"Thanks."

Tuck left the apartment and paused for a moment, glancing behind him at the door he'd just closed. Was there something more he could do for his friend? It obviously wasn't a topic Steve wanted to discuss, since he'd only just told Tuck about it.

All he could do was be there if Steve needed something. Keys in hand, he waited for the elevator and caught a ride to the first floor, smiling at the others in the car with him.

He typed the address he wanted into his GPS and got on his way. When he arrived, he parked before the tall building and walked into the lobby. It was mostly empty except for the two men who sat at a desk in the middle of the lobby entrance.

"Can we help you, sir?"

"I'm here to speak to Ms Greene of Prometheus Protections."

The man looked him over. "Fifth floor."

"Thank you."

He took his time walking along the spotless dark tiled floor. The set-up was nice and everything matched. According to the board beside the elevators, there was quite a variety of businesses filling up this building.

In the elevator, he pressed the button for the fifth floor and rested against the wall as they headed up. Prometheus Protections had half of the entire floor. Across from them was a dental practice.

Once out of the car, he looked both directions. The dentist's door was very plain and had the name on it. To the right, Prometheus Protections had their logo on the door. He went to the door and opened it.

An Asian woman sat at a desk near the entrance and looked up when he entered. Behind her was another door that led down a hallway. The sitting area wasn't that big but it was nice. It didn't take a genius to see most of what happened at this place went on beyond that door he'd bet anything was locked.

"Good morning, sir, welcome to Prometheus Protections. May I assist you?"

She wore no nametag and her suit was black. Her hair, drawn back in a tight bun, highlighted her features.

"I'm Mr Carter. I worked with Ms Greene yesterday and wondered if I could have a word with her."

"I'll see if she's available." She gestured with her hand. "Please, have a seat."

He did and waited. The woman spoke too low to be overheard and he wanted to shift beneath the heavy weight of her stare.

Barely a minute later, Ariel strode from the hallway behind the woman. The door clicked and she continued forwards. Her gaze narrowed slightly when she met his. He rose to his feet as she gave the woman at the desk a smile and stepped past.

Another suit. This one was a pants suit and was cream and navy. She stopped right in front of him. He had to work hard to keep his physical reaction in check. Professional as hell she may be, but he found her hot as fuck. The way she wore her suits did as much to him as the way she filled out shorts and T-shirt. And like then, he wanted her now.

"Mr Carter. Is there something I can help you with?"

Chapter Four

Ariel wanted to punch him. What the crap was he doing here? When Connie had called her and told her a Mr Carter was here to see her, she'd prayed it was another Carter. Her prayers had gone unanswered. She waited for an answer but he didn't speak.

"Mr Carter?"

He blinked and refocused on her eyes. Good, because her nipples weren't handling his attention well.

"Sorry to bother you, Ms Greene, but can we talk?"

Damn him, damn him, damn him. While she longed to stomp her foot and yell they couldn't, she knew that wasn't allowed. "Sure, let's go to my office." She gestured behind her. "Just sign in."

She stared at his ass as he filled out the sheet and got a visitor's badge from Connie. *Be strong. Be strong.* Yesterday had been a mix of heaven and hell. The sex had been incredible but the realization of what she'd done had sent her spiraling back to hell. This addiction she had to him wasn't healthy in the least.

When he was ready, she moved by him to the door. She gripped the handle and paused until the square hooked to the inside of her pocket vibrated. Then she pulled and waved him through.

They didn't speak as she led him down the hall to her office. With another hand gesture, she had him enter first. She closed the door behind him and allowed herself one final stare at his ass.

In her chair, she leaned back and drummed her fingers on the smooth wooden top. "What do you need, Tuck?"

He sat leisurely in a chair across from her. "Nice place you have here. What's the lock on the door to get back here?"

"It's one of the things we offer. Looking for a protection service?"

"Do you also do personal protection?"

"Yes we do." She picked up her pencil and tapped it on the papers she'd been working on at the time she'd received the call. "I'm busy, Tuck. What?"

"Richard wanted me to check and see how things were coming."

"And you couldn't have asked that when I called you back yesterday?"

His shrug was shameless. "Didn't know then." He pushed to his feet and walked to the wall lined with pictures to the right of her desk. "Is this Roxi?"

She turned in her chair and saw the one he pointed at. "Yes. That's Roxi. We're in Uganda in that shot. Are you wanting to see all the pictures or can we get to work showing you what we've done so I can get back to it and finish it up?"

He turned quickly and her breath hitched. Damn him for being so hot.

"Ready to work," he said. He began to draw the chair closer but she shook her head.

"We'll go to one of the large rooms where this stuff can be spread out."

The gleam in his eyes had her pussy creaming. It was the one he'd had while he'd taken her over and over at the construction site.

"I do like having room to work," he said.

She cursed her traitorous body. Even now, she could feel it gravitating toward him. Her lust for him had been bad before but she'd not known what she'd been missing. Now she knew and every single cell inside her wanted to be in the know *again*.

Without responding, she led the way to the room she wanted to use. Slater met them in the hall.

"Everything okay?" he asked.

"Yes, sir. This is Mr Carter, I met with him yesterday and his boss has sent him to see where we are at. I was taking him to Room Three to do just that."

"Okay." He reached out his hand. "Nice to meet you, Mr Carter. I'm Mr McKenzie."

Ariel waited with impatience as they finished their greetings. Slater sent her a look she knew meant to visit him later. Finally they made it to Room Three.

"Take a seat," she ordered as she walked to the computer keyboard by her chair. Typing in her code, she accessed the file and up it came. A three-dimensional image of the museum appeared in the middle of the table. She touched another button and the lights dimmed considerably in the room, allowing the image to be more easily viewed.

"Wow," Tuck said, leaning forward. "Call me suitably impressed, Ariel. Truly. This is awesome."

She ignored the warm feeling that accompanied his compliment. "This is what we've worked out."

Ariel gave him the spiel that caught him up to where she was currently at. Different colors were highlighted at times to correspond to what she was explaining. Surprisingly, Tuck didn't interrupt with comments about their time fucking, but he did ask questions that were logical and made good sense.

She leaned back and thumped her pencil on the table. The lights remained low and the image continued to hover over the glossy surface.

"I'll be finished with the rest tomorrow if you need to go over it all once it's entirely completed."

"I'm fucking impressed. Who's going to be coming to install?"

"We'll send a team of four. They won't get in the way of you or your men, so don't worry about that. They're good and fast. It won't take them long to put all this into effect."

"Seems so complex," he commented.

"It is on one hand. On the other, it's not. Probably just seems that way since it's not for a house but a museum, and we wanted to insure that any of the artefacts they bring in and have either on display or in the back are well protected."

"I'm at a loss for words, Ariel. Truly I am. Y'all have done an outstanding job. I know Richard will be pleased and if the museum isn't then they're stupid. What did they think of it, by the way?"

"I spoke to Gerald yesterday and he just said to get it done and make sure nothing was delayed with the opening. They have some big exhibit coming to be part of the opening day gala thing they're holding."

She relaxed as they spoke. This was the Tuck she remembered. The one who was easy to talk to, not the one who stole her panties and fucked her with raw abandon until it hurt to walk.

Shit. I have got to stop thinking about all those times. Each and every one. The multiple and numerous orgasms he's given me.

"You going to the gala?"

"Me?" She took deep breaths, desperate to lower her core temperature. "Not sure why I'd go. Unless it was something I really wanted to see but then I'd have to be able to afford the tickets even."

He grunted and she gestured with her chin.

"You?"

"No clue. Opening day is a long way off."

"True. It is a bit out there."

He rose and walked around the table to take the seat beside her. Swallowing, she focused on the image instead of him.

"Why do things have to be difficult between us?"

"They don't. Let me alone and we'll be fine."

"You still going on about that ashamed bullshit?" he snapped.

"I don't judge you and how you react in the flings you partake in, Tuck. Why do you think you have the right to nose into how I handle it?"

He whipped her chair toward him. "Because *your* fling had to do with *me*. You don't get to treat me like a leper and avoid your own apartment."

Anger spiked along her spine and she matched him glare for glare. "Wow, I'm pretty sure you're not my parent and therefore have no right to tell me anything about how I act."

"Like a scared wuss. I thought you said you were a Marine."

She narrowed her gaze. "Watch the words that come out of your mouth next. I don't take kindly to slander against the Corps."

"I thought they were supposed to be some of the bravest."

"We are," she replied instantly. "One has nothing to do with the other."

"Bullshit." He jerked on the chair. "You're running."

"From what?" Her fingers dug into the sides of the armrests. "I have *nothing* to run from."

"Don't lie to either of us, Ariel Greene. I bet you're wet right now and if I shoved my fingers into you, they'd come out covered in your cream."

"Sex is sex, Tuck. I can get it anywhere and so long as the man is talented, I'll be wet. I never said I wasn't attracted to you, so that's a pointless argument." Her heart pounded so hard she wondered if it would punch through her ribs and fall out onto her pants.

"You're still running."

Now she was getting pissed. *Does he have to keep pushing this issue? Can we not feel the need to address the fact that's exactly what I'm doing?* "From what?" Cripes, when did her voice escalate so? "You've made it perfectly clear how you treat women. You go through them like you're eating a bag of chips. One right after another. Who's the one running?"

"So this is on me because I didn't have a steady girlfriend when we fucked?" His tone dropped dangerously low.

"Had there been a girlfriend in your life, *that* wouldn't have happened," she snarled.

"How many batteries do you go through calling my name again?"

Ice coated her heart and she drew on the strength that had got her through Boot. With a barely there blink she stared at him, shoving the humiliation she had into a small dark corner where it wouldn't see the light of day.

"More than I should be. If that's all, Mr Carter, I have work to continue."

He shoved back with a sharp, "Whatever."

It wasn't hard to see his anger and frustration but right now, she didn't care. Her own were surging with the force of a powerful rip tide and she was having a hard time keeping herself from being pulled under.

Ariel moved around and pressed a button. Within seconds, two men dressed in suits stepped into the room. "Yes, Ms Greene?"

She looked them over. The twins on staff—Brandon and Landon Towers.

Landon had spoken. She'd learned to tell them apart over the time she'd worked here. It hadn't been easy for they had taken great pleasure in trying to fool her.

"Mr Carter was just leaving. Escort him out, please."

Tuck glared at her but she didn't care. This was her place—she didn't have to face a damn thing if she didn't want to.

"Yes, ma'am." Landon again. "Sir, if you will come with us."

The words, while spoken respectfully, truly offered no option. Tuck seemed to realize that and shook his head in her direction as he went with them. She made a big production of shutting off the display as he left the room, so she wouldn't watch. Then she returned to her office and after a long drink of cold water, got back to work. Doing her damnedest to ignore the desire coursing through her body courtesy of one Tuck Carter.

* * * *

"She tossed me out. Had two men there who escorted me to the door like I would cause a problem."

Steve sat across from him at the table they'd claimed the moment they had entered the sports bar. A bottle of beer dangled from his fingertips as he stared at Tuck.

"I'm confused, Tuck. What did you think was going to happen?"

"Why is it so hard for her to think of us as being together?"

Steve blinked a few times. "Is that what this is about? You want to date her?"

He leaned back and crossed his arms. "Is that such a ridiculous notion to you?"

"Given your track record? Yes."

"I want more, Steve."

"Obviously." His retort was dry.

Tuck flipped him off and drank some of his beer. "I didn't want anything more with the others. It's her I want it with. Why is that so hard for her to understand?"

"Have you told her this? Or was it more of an 'I fucked you numerous times, I bet you're wet now' kind of thing?"

Tuck shrugged.

Steve laughed even as he shook his head. "There's your problem. You want her, you should tell her. Better yet, ask her out on a date."

"And how do you propose I do that when she's avoiding me like the plague. Hell, like I'm the one who gave it to her."

Steve rolled his eyes and waved for another drink. "Poor, poor Tuck. Not used to having to put out energy to get a woman. Wonder what that says about the women you're usually with."

"You know, you truly can be an asshole."

"More than you know, man. More than you know. Look, Ariel's not been talking to me either so I don't know what to tell you. But I suggest you ask, and I do mean *ask* her out on a real date. Treat her like a woman and not like an item you'd just like to fuck."

Tuck rested his elbows on the table and rolled his bottle on the bottom as he thought about the past week. He'd not once seen Ariel. Occasionally he saw her vehicle in their parking garage, but never her. Woman had gone dark. He didn't like it at all. He reached for his burger and bit in. This would take a good deal of planning but Steve was right. He wanted something more than that bedroom fling and he had to stop looking at her like sex was all he wished for.

He wanted more sex, definitely. But it was more than that. She'd gotten under his skin—had since he first saw her and had that thought of lilacs surround him with its gentle and refreshing scent.

They'd played this cat and mouse game for over a year and a half, the teasing becoming more and more sexual between them. Yet at the same time they could just hang at sporting events together and have a great time. She understood the rules and didn't ask annoying questions through the whole thing. Another bonus was that she'd never asked him to go shopping with her.

Their actual sleeping together had flipped a switch in his mind and all he could focus on was her. He wanted to be able to call her his. Go to sleep with her in his arms. *Shit, it's like I'm thinking forever.*

With a mental reprimand, he focused back on the game on one of the many flat screens around the establishment. He and Steve hung out until late before making their way back to the apartment. Her car was gone—that was the first thing he noticed. The second was that someone was waiting for him.

Daisy. *Ah, shit.*

She pushed away from the wall and sashayed over to place her hands on his chest. "Hello, Tuck," she purred.

"What are you doing here, Daisy?"

Steve waved and gave him a wicked grin as he slipped inside the building. *Bastard.* Tuck stared at the woman whom he had made the mistake of sleeping with. She was dressed in the same way she had been the first time they'd met—incredibly short shorts, a belly-exposing cut-off shirt and stilettos. This time, however, it did nothing for him.

She tucked a curl of her hair—now dark red—behind her ear and stepped closer. "You didn't answer any of my calls."

"Nope, I didn't. Thought you would have gotten the hint from that."

Her eyes widened in surprise. "I thought we had something."

"It was a one-night stand. That's it. Nothing more, nothing less." Yes, he was being an ass but he didn't need her hanging around thinking there was more to what they'd shared.

She faltered but regained her composure quickly. Dragging her tongue along her lips—an act he realized was supposed to be sexy—she stepped closer to him and reinitiated physical contact. The tips of her nails began to dig into his skin and he frowned, removing her touch.

"We were good together," she said.

He exhaled noisily. "I said before, one-night stand. There's nothing more there. Get it through your head. Goodnight, Daisy." He walked around her then entered the building. Shaking his head, he made his way to the elevator. More proof that Steve and Ariel were right. He had way too many confrontations like this. And it had to stop.

I don't want anyone but Ariel now, so it will.

On their floor, he cast a glance to her door and continued to his. Had her vehicle been there, he would have pounded until she answered. But it wasn't, so he didn't.

"Yes, sure. We can do that for you. Don't worry, it'll be taken care of," Steve assured.

"Who was that?" Tuck asked when Steve hung up.

"Ariel. She asked me to look after her plants for her."

His eyebrows converged and he closed the door behind him. "Why? Where is she?"

"She's gone for two weeks."

"To where?"

The security had been added to the museum and the men doing the installation were, as she'd said, good at what they did. But why would she leave before everything had been finalized?

"This is her two weeks of service. She's in the Marine Reserve. This is her full-drill status."

He calmed down a bit, remembering she had somewhere to be one weekend a month. "How are you going to do that if we don't have the key to her place anymore?"

"Oh, I have a key."

"You? You have a key to her place?"

"Yes, she put it in the mailbox, I picked it up earlier today when I got the mail."

Tuck held out his hand. "I'll take care of her plants."

"Nope, sorry man. She asked me to do it. I don't need you over there sleeping in her bed because it smells like her."

Tuck muttered some expletives and went to his room. This day hadn't gone at all as planned. Seated before his computer, he pulled up the plans for his house and spent the next few hours working on them. He was close to having them just right, but it wasn't quite there yet.

* * * *

At the construction site the next day, he stood with several of the men as they took their break. He stared at the building—it had come along beautifully. From where they were on the roof, he watched the landscaping guys smoothing out some parts that hadn't been able to be done while they were trucking in and out materials.

His cell rang and he answered it. "Hello?"

"Pierce. Can you come meet me?"

"Sure, Richard. What's up?"

"I'll shoot you the address. Come as soon as you can."

"Okay, I'll leave right away." He ended the call and looked at Stan. "Richard called me away. You guys are on your own."

The men whooped and hollered. "Party time!"

He laughed as he made his way down off the roof. His phone vibrated with the announcement of a text but he didn't look at it until he made it to his truck. Tossing his hard hat into the back seat, he climbed in then unclipped his phone to see where he was to go.

It took him nearly an hour to get to where Richard wanted to meet him. After parking beside the man's

Escalade, he hopped out. Richard waited there in a suit and, shoving his hands in his pockets, Tuck joined him on the side of the hill.

"What's up?"

"Beautiful, isn't it?"

He took in the scenery—rolling hills and grass with some trees dotting the landscape. "Yes. What's this for? Are we building here?"

"Maybe." Richard sighed heavily and Tuck glanced at him.

"So I drove out here to what?"

Richard gave a small bark of laughter. "Always so straightforward, Pierce. I've admired that about you. How are your plans coming along for your own house?"

He smiled. "Nearly there. Final tweaking right now, so to speak."

"Looking forward to seeing them. You have an amazing eye for this stuff and I told you this before when you first came to me with wanting to be an architect—I want to help you accomplish your dream."

"And you have been. I get to do more than just follow the plans and build. I have a say in things and get to go to meetings you've had with clients. It's all been wonderful. Thank you."

"Have you given any thought to where you want to build your home?"

Tuck rocked back on his heels. "Nope. Can't say that I have. I do enjoy it here in San Antonio."

"Amount of land you want?"

"A few acres perhaps. Haven't given that much thought either. What's with the questions, Richard?"

"Indulge an old man."

"Old? You do more than I do daily. Old is the last thing I would call you."

"Trust me, I feel my age some days."

Tuck glanced at his friend and mentor. Nothing was given away on that face, so he stared out across the land. It *was* beautiful.

What plans the man had wouldn't be revealed until he was ready. Tuck wasn't usually the most patient of people but he had enough respect for this man to wait.

"I think you're ready for your own company," Richard said eventually. "And I want to help you get it going."

Nope, he'd not been expecting that at all.

Chapter Five

Crack!

The ball flew off the end of her bat. Ariel dropped it and hauled ass to first then rounding the base, she continued toward second as she saw the ball drop past the center fielder's head and subsequently his glove. She'd underestimated his throwing arm, however, and she slid head first into a safe—thankfully—call from the second base umpire.

"Way to go, Ariel!" the cries came from the bench.

She held out an arm, hand up until the ump gave her the nod and she finally got to her feet, stepping off the base she'd just slid over. Shaking the dirt from her uniform, she winced at the pain in her side. She removed her batting gloves and shin guard then met the first base coach who took them from her.

With a fist bump her commanding officer smiled at her. "Great job, Greene," he said.

"Thanks." Another twinge of pain she ignored as she jogged back to the base.

"Lucky hit, Greene." The words came from behind her.

"Don't be jealous just because you're zero for two today, Haskell."

Jared Haskell stepped into her periphery and sent her a grin. "We'll see about that next time I'm up. How've you been?"

They hadn't seen each other in a while—being sent to other places during these two weeks, this was the first time she'd run into him.

"Good, good. You? How's the wife and kids?"

"Getting bigger all the time. All of them. Sharon is pregnant again."

She laughed. "Congratulations, man. Why do you sound surprised by that? Surely by now you get the concept of the birds and the bees, and what happens when you do that dirty nasty thing in bed."

He flashed a grin and began backing up. "See, that's where my problem comes in. We rarely use the bed."

"I didn't need to know that," she cried as more laughter bubbled from her throat.

She loved the two weeks she got to spend with her fellow Marines. Some days she wondered why she'd gotten out in the first place. Maybe she should get back in—something to think about, for sure.

Ariel put her attention back on the game as First Lieutenant Gainesly got up in the batter's box. This woman had played softball in high school and her school had never lost their division while she'd been there. She was wicked good with a bat, so Ariel was expecting a hit.

Gainesly didn't disappoint. The ball launched off the end of her bat and Ariel watched it sail toward right field. When the man there caught it, she tagged up and hauled ass to third, sliding into this one as well.

This time tears sprang to her eyes as she waited for the okay to step from the base. A bit slower to her feet this time, she still managed a fist bump with the third base coach.

"You okay there, Greene?" Sergeant Mallory asked.

"Yes, ma'am. Think I slid into second a bit hard. I'll be fine."

"Okay. If it still hurts tonight, get it checked out."

"Yes, ma'am."

* * * *

The rest of the afternoon flew by with speedy fashion. Ariel's team won by one, which gave them bragging rights until the next unit game. The cookout was just what she needed, loud, brash and totally how Marines did it. Music blared and as she went in for another hamburger, her phone rang.

"Greene."

"Ariel, it's me, Tuck. Don't hang up."

Tuck. That name. That voice. The naughty places they took her imagination.

"What can I do for you?" She winked at the grill master who put a burger on the bun she'd opened on her plate.

"I know you're due to be home in a few days. I want to take you out on a date. A real date."

The plate wobbled in her hand. "A date?" Her voice sounded like a squeak.

"Yes. So will you, Ariel Greene, go on a date with me?"

"A date?" she asked again.

"Yes. Not to a ballgame either or a sports bar. Dressy. Somewhere nice where we're not shouting to be heard or having beer spilled on us by the row above or tossed on us from the ones below."

Her mind began to list the reasons this would be a bad idea. Her mouth, however, moved and replied, "Sure."

Tuck was quiet for a moment. "Wonderful. I'll see you when you get back then, Ariel. Be safe." He hung up.

She slipped her phone back in her pocket and went to fix her burger, sort of dazed. Tuck Carter had just asked her out on an actual date. He didn't usually do that with women he'd already taken to bed. She could count on one hand the number of times she'd seen him with the same woman more than once.

* * * *

It was late when she entered her building. She yawned as she got her mail, disgusted with the amount of crap that had arrived. *Should have had them get my mail again as well as water my plants.* Then she made her way to the stairs and began climbing.

Regretting her choice to walk as she made it up the last section before her floor, she heard a man talking. Steve. He didn't sound happy and she nearly went back down to give him privacy. Her legs and exhausted brain made the final decision. She didn't have anything left, all the way around.

Ariel readjusted her sea bag on one shoulder and tromped up the final few steps. Steve seemed shocked to see her. She gave him a small wave and went immediately to her door, slipping inside as soon as it was unlocked.

She shut it behind her, dropped the bag and stumbled to her bed after a brief stop in the bathroom. Unfortunately, just because she'd been delayed didn't mean her rousing hour for work had changed. When her alarm sounded, she'd managed almost two hours of sleep.

"That was definitely not enough sleep." She went to her living room and grabbed her previously discarded bag. After emptying it, she showered then picked out a skirt suit to wear as she dried. Coffee in her travel mug, she shouldered her purse and walked, fully dressed for work, out of the door.

Beyoncé accompanied her into work as her latest CD played in Ariel's vehicle. Past the gate guard, she drove up to the fifth floor and parked in her usual spot. Her drink was nearly finished and she made a mental note to fix more as soon as she got in. Connie was there as she entered.

"You do know it's okay to call in after a two week stint like that, right?" The petite woman arched an eyebrow at her.

Ariel shrugged. "What fun would that be?"

Connie rolled her eyes. "I figured as much. That being said, I started your coffee pot since I figured you could use a bit extra. Messages are on your desk in order of importance, top being the most critical to return."

"You do know you don't have to do those things for me, Connie."

"I know, but I like you so I don't mind."

"I can't tell you how much it's appreciated, either."

The women passed through to the back hall. Connie easily kept pace despite their height difference. Ariel wasn't fooled—she knew Connie could kick her ass. Connie was more than the first face you saw upon entering Prometheus Protections—she was also Slater's personal bodyguard.

"Tell me about that hottie, Mr Carter."

"What's to tell?" *Christ, I even think about him and my body flushes heat.*

"Please. Slater may not see how things are there but I sure did. Now dish."

Ariel entered her office, smiling when the rich scent of freshly brewed coffee met her with welcoming arms. "Not gonna let it go, are you?"

"Hell, no. We don't open for an hour so I'm not needed up front. I've been in a dry spell, have to live vicariously through you. So give me deets and make them juicy."

She laughed. "Sometimes I forget we're the same age, Connie."

Connie joined her and sat in one of the chairs. "I know, most do. Come on, do tell. I need to hear. How is he?"

Ariel topped off her mug and sat after putting her purse in the bottom drawer of her desk. "Unfuckingbelieveable."

Connie squealed and slid the chair closer. "How did it happen? At the work site? Somewhere dirty where he took you against a wall and you didn't care? Or was it after a nice dinner?" She narrowed her eyes. "Work site. You have freak written all over you."

She snorted and curved her fingers around the mug. "He's my neighbor, has been since I moved out here. We went to a Missions game then out. Back at the building I told him"—she shook her head in disbelief—"I told him if he only knew how many batteries I went through because of him."

"You didn't!" Her eyes were wide.

"Not one of my finest moments. Then I kissed him and woke up in his bed."

"How was he?" She leaned forward even more.

"It hurt to walk the following day."

Connie erupted with laughter and clapped. "Now, the work site. Don't keep me in suspense. You two got your freak on there, didn't you?"

Ariel ducked her head and Connie howled louder.

"I knew it. I knew it! I need details. How many times?"

Ariel blew out a breath. "Six."

"Oh God, I need me some of that."

"Some of what?" Slater's question entered their conversation.

It was like a switch had been thrown. Connie stopped laughing, her expression returning to the no-nonsense one she normally sported.

"Coffee," Connie deadpanned. She rose and smoothed down her black suit coat. "Glad you made it back safe, Ariel."

"Dinner tonight, Connie. After work. You and me."

Her smile was fleeting. "Sounds good." She left, skirting Slater.

"Something I said?" her boss asked.

She sipped some coffee and shrugged. "Just talking about sex—she probably didn't want you to hear."

He held up his hands and shook his head. "I don't want to know."

Hiding her smirk, she replied, "You asked."

"Connie wouldn't talk about sex. And I don't want to think about it even if she did."

Apparently Slater only saw one side of Connie.

"Believe what you will."

Slater backed out of her office. "Swing by when you finish your stuff here."

"You got it."

Work was busy and passed quickly. New clients, new accounts and some to close out.

Connie buzzed her. "Yes, Connie?"

"There's a Mr Schaffer to see you."

Damn. "I'll be right there."

"Very good, ma'am."

Ariel replaced the receiver and slipped her feet back into her pumps she'd kicked off earlier, groaning. Thomas Schaffer had been a pain in her side since the walk-through at the museum.

I'm so not looking forward to this.

Ensuring her badge and pin were clipped to her outfit, she made her way to the front. She passed through the door visitors couldn't get by without a member of Prometheus escorting them and saw him. He stood by the window, staring out over San Antonio. His three thousand dollar suit fitted him well and did absolutely nothing for her.

"Mr Schaffer, what can I do for you?" Her voice carried to him and he turned, although she'd bet he had been watching for her reflection in the window. With a practiced smile on her face, she waited for him to speak.

He didn't right away, just watched her in a way that made her skin crawl.

"Think about where you want to go for dinner. My only request — make sure there's alcohol served, I have a feeling after this I'm going to need a drink. Or five," she whispered to Connie as she went by her to meet him.

* * * *

Tuck stared at the downpour that streamed by the window. Behind him, the radio talked about the increased threat of tornados and he shook his head before picking up his radio.

"That's it, guys, we're done for the day. Pack it in, go home and be safe."

He waited for everyone to leave before doing one last walk-through of the place, ensuring all was as secure as he could make it. There was just no point in continuing to work at a site that had so many projectiles if they were talking tornado.

Standing near the front, he dialed Richard and told him he'd sent the men home. Then he dashed through the downpour to his truck and hopped in. After passing the gate, he jumped out and locked it before getting back into his vehicle, soaking wet. It wasn't pretty out there, that was for sure.

He hadn't seen Ariel yet and he knew she'd been back a day at least. Tomorrow was their date—he'd put the note on her door last night and when he'd left this morning for work, it had been gone. He was looking forward to it.

After stopping off at the grocery store, he made it back to his place. The skies had gotten even darker and the rain came harder as he ran inside, carrying the bags. Shaking his head to remove some of the rain, he eyed the elevator and got in with a couple from the third floor. They exchanged pleasantries then he fell silent.

He got off on his floor and went to his apartment, casting a look over his shoulder to her door. It was shut tight.

Inside his place, he changed into some dry clothes before putting away the groceries. He heard laughter outside the door and went to look. Ariel stood there soaked from head to foot with another woman. He almost didn't recognize her but did after a moment. She'd been at Prometheus Protections behind the front desk. Then, she'd looked severe. Now, in jeans and a T-shirt she seemed more approachable.

"Hello, Ariel," he said, leaning against the doorframe, hooking his ankles and crossing his arms. "You look a bit wet."

The women shared a look and snorted. "Just a bit," she quipped. "Tuck, this is Connie. Connie, this is Tuck."

Connie grinned at him and he wondered if he'd just passed some kind of test. "So nice to meet you again, Tuck."

"And you. So, what are you ladies up to this stormy afternoon?"

"We're going to have pizza and continue talking about sex like we did at dinner last night." Ariel gave him a smirk. "Care to join us?"

Now, he might want to spend as much time with her as he could, but even he knew better. "I think I should pass."

"Are you sure?" Connie asked. "We'd love to get your opinion on things."

Yep, Ariel had told her friend about them. *At least I ranked important enough to do that.* "Again, I think I'll pass. I have some work of my own to do."

Ariel shrugged. "Suit yourself. Not sure what there's to be scared of, but hey, if you are..." She blinked. "You are."

He walked across to stand before his dripping goddess. "I would be insane to claim otherwise. Talking sex with two women—no thank you." He kissed her, reveling in the taste of her. "Don't forget about tomorrow."

"I haven't forgotten," she muttered.

"You two have fun now." He strode back to his apartment and shut the door before his cock overruled his good sense. "Pizza sounds good, though."

Tuck searched their freezer and pulled one out for himself. As it cooked, he got to work on his house — Richard had asked him to finish the plans so he could see them. The man was still talking about helping him get off the ground with his own business. Tuck was going to take advantage and see what happened.

Occasionally, however, his attention and gaze drifted to the door, as if he could see through into Ariel's apartment and whatever the women were doing. His perverted mind had them having pillow fights and other things, clad in very little clothing, if any.

He pulled the pizza out when Steve came in, as soaked as everyone else seemed to be this day.

"Hey, man."

"What's going on at Ariel's?" he asked.

"She and a co-worker are having pizza and talking sex. Or so that's what they told me when they invited me to participate in the discussion."

Steve shook his head. "I see you made the right choice."

"Man, even I know better than to do that. But the pizza sounded good so I made one."

"Let me get into something that isn't like I fell into the Gulf of Mexico and I'll be right back."

Ten minutes later, they were eating in the living room.

"So how are things going with the new venture?" Steve asked.

"I've been working on finishing up the house this afternoon. Richard asked to see the completed plans. He's been on me nearly daily since he took me out to see that parcel of land. So I don't want to keep him waiting anymore. Don't get many ops like this to have part of the day off. I'm taking advantage of it."

"Excellent. I looked into the building for you and brought back the details."

Tuck leaned forward. "Do you think it will work?"

Steve was a realtor but also had the benefit of being a real estate attorney.

"I liked the area and the building looked sound from a contractor's point of view."

"I personally don't like the lease they're trying to sign someone to but I brought it for you to look at. After you go over it, we can talk about the points which strike me as wrong and something you'd want to have changed."

Tuck ate some more of his pepperoni and sausage pizza. "I trust you, Steve. If you say there are problems, I'm not going to argue that. You know the terminology so much better than I do."

Steve reached for his beer and thunder cracked overhead. "They may be willing to renegotiate so it's still an option."

"I want what's best, not something that's doable." He was utilizing Steve's expertise in locating a building for his own business. "There are only a few more for you to look into that I'd even consider buying."

"Okay. We can still go over it and see what you think. Or I can move on to the other properties."

"Good idea."

"Any thought as to why he showed you that other piece of property?"

"None. Did you find out anything on it?"

"Just that Richard owns it. There's almost two hundred acres there in his name. He owns a lot of property scattered around this state."

Tuck hadn't known about that—apparently there were a few things he didn't know about his boss.

"He's also got a lot of buildings for rent, Tuck. We could look at some of them, too. The list is also in the stack of papers there."

The lights flickered a few times then went out. "Damn," Tuck said, getting up to find some flashlights. Even though it wasn't night out, the sky was too dark to offer any visibility.

Rumbles shook the building and once he'd found the flashlights, he went back to the living room. Steve was standing there with one as well.

"Should we check on the women?"

Thank God, Steve had recommended that because he didn't want to look like a sucker who couldn't stand being away from Ariel. "Sure."

"Yeah, that sounds like you'd not been thinking about it at all. Come on, you lovelorn puppy."

They left and crossed the hall to knock. Ariel opened the door and he switched off his flashlight. Her place was well lit, or at least the living area was—two lanterns offered light.

"Hello," she said. "Come to check on us?"

"Yes."

"Sweet. Hi, Steve. Come on in."

They entered and she shut the door behind them.

"Connie, this is Steve. Steve, Connie. And you remember Tuck from a while ago."

Connie walked into view from the small kitchen holding a pitcher of margaritas. "Hello. At least the drinks were finished before we lost power. Are you two joining us?"

He shared a glance with Steve. "Yes."

Ariel cocked an eyebrow. "Even if we're talking about sex?"

"Still?" he questioned.

Both women laughed. "Oh, you poor deluded man. We can talk that all day and then some." Ariel gestured them to join them and he took a chair while Steve took another. The women sat together on the sofa.

Connie was a cute little thing but it was Ariel who continually captured his attention. She wore a pair of shorts that did intense things to his libido and a white tank top that showed off her darker skin to perfection. Connie had dressed something similar. Both women had their hair up in ponytails and he found himself staring at the muscles in their arms. He knew about Ariel's strength, but Connie was a bit of a surprise to him. He'd written her off as a petite little thing—now he wondered.

They ate and drank as the storm raged around them. Thankfully there were no tornados. It was after ten that night when they finally broke it up and headed to their apartment.

"Thanks, Ariel," Steve said giving her a hug. "Lovely to meet you, Connie."

"And you." She waved at them and Steve propelled him to the door.

"Let it go, man. You have your date tomorrow."

So he did. And he had a sleepless night and a restless day. When he left his apartment that night for their date, he took a deep breath. In one hand he held a bouquet of flowers and he rapped sharply on the wood with the other. He hadn't seen her since he'd left her apartment the previous day.

"Come on in," she called out.

He pushed in then closed the door behind him. Her place was spotless, no trace of the drinks they'd had yesterday or the food they'd eaten. The lanterns were nowhere to be seen either.

"I'll be right there, Tuck."

"No rush. Where'd you get those lanterns you had last night?"

"Marine Corps."

He should have known. He licked his lips and tried to calm his nerves. It shouldn't be bothering him so much but he felt as he had taking Wendy Mackrel to prom. All nervous and unsure. He wanted to wipe his hands off on his pants so his palms wouldn't be sweaty.

Her heels sounded on the floor and he looked toward her bedroom. One second there was just the doorway, the next, Ariel stood there. All the air rushed from his lungs.

"Holy shit. You're beautiful."

His words brought a small smile to her face, erasing the uncertainty there. "Is this okay?"

He could barely find the words. "Perfect," he croaked.

Her dress was a changing blend of purple and blue. The cowl neckline and halter top offered him a tantalizing sneak peek at her full breasts beneath the material. He knew the asymmetrical skirt would be the death of him tonight—it was knee length on one side and floor length on the other. She had on stilettos that criss-crossed up her calves. Small stones added sparkle when the light hit the material. Sexy goddess. Her hair was unconfined and flowed around her shoulders.

"Wonderful," she replied. "Shall we?"

"Yes." Lord, he needed to manage more than one word responses or the evening would be rough. He shoved the flowers in her direction. "Flowers."

A smile graced her face, a real full one this time. "Those are beautiful, thank you." She walked toward him and took the lilies. "I'll just put them in water and we can go."

He couldn't talk, he was too busy watching her ass in the dress. When she returned to stand before him, he raked his gaze over her once more.

"Ready?"

She picked up her clutch. "Let's go."

"One thing first." He finally was able to get the words out.

"What's that?"

He turned her to him and kissed her. Thrust his tongue deep into her mouth. A moan slipped up from her throat and he took that as well. His cock pressed insistently against his slacks and he drew away from her, knowing he had to or they'd not make it to dinner.

"You're absolutely gorgeous, Ariel."

Chapter Six

Ariel glanced askew at Tuck as they made their way to his truck. His black suit, classically handsome, amplified the width of his broad shoulders and emphasized the leanness of his waist and hips. *Damn, he's fine.*

His hair was sexily disarrayed, giving him the appearance of someone who'd run their fingers through the silken locks — an act she would love to do. And the offer nearly slid free of her mouth.

He held the passenger door for her and she brushed against him as she stepped up. She'd been in his vehicle maybe twice before. It was totally him — a ball cap on the dash, some ticket stubs on the seat between them. She was glad he hadn't tried to make it perfectly clean before she got there, it wouldn't have been him. Not that it was dirty, but it wasn't spotless.

"Where are we going?" She buckled her seatbelt.

"Hanson's." He closed his door and started the truck.

Staring out of the window, she nodded. "I've heard they have really good food."

"So you've never been there?" He got them out of the parking lot and onto the streets of San Antonio.

"Nope."

"Good."

"Have you? Wait, why good?" She canted her head to the side so she could see him better.

Pure sex rolled off the grin he sported. "I was there once, for a business dinner with some clients. And it's good because then your first time is with me." He met her gaze head on and the heat in his eyes sent an influx of desire through her. "I happen to like it that way."

Lordy, she was ready to melt into a puddle. He was already a first for a few things. *Not telling him that, though.* "I see," her response fell.

The ride to the restaurant was completed in silence aside from some soft classic rock he had on. Pulling up to the front of the restaurant, she smiled at the valet who opened her door for her as she undid her belt.

"Good evening, ma'am."

"Good evening." She allowed the young man to assist her out.

Moments later, Tuck strode around the hood of his truck, gave her a smile and offered her his arm. She took it willingly and relaxed along his side. Together, they entered the establishment and went up to the maître d'.

"Name, sir?"

"Pierce Carter."

She smiled over the use of his full name. It was difficult for her to imagine him as anything but Tuck.

The man made a mark on his paper and waved over a woman who also wore a tuxedo. The words they exchanged were two low for her to overhear.

"If you'll follow me." The woman gave a smile and led the way.

"You have a suspicious look on your face," he whispered in her ear. "What's going on in that head of yours?"

"I'm not used to hearing you called Pierce. I don't see you as one. Just interesting is all."

"You don't see me as one?"

"No. Tuck fits you so much better. Pierce seems, oh, I don't know, stuffy or something like that."

His chuckle had her smiling. "If it helps, I don't see myself as a Pierce either."

Tuck held her chair for her and brushed a kiss along her cheek as he pushed her in. Their table was by a wall that had water rivulets streaming down it, creating a lovely sound. Soft lighting behind the water circulated hues every minute and added to the atmosphere.

Sleek. Elegant. Way nicer than anything she'd attended recently. *Not even just recently. I've not been out anywhere nice in a while. Not to this degree.* Roxi's wedding had been lovely but they didn't get to any places like this.

"What do you think?"

She stared at him across the white linen tablecloth and the two lit tapers in silver engraved holders.

"Thank you for bringing me." She gave him a smile. "It's lovely. And I am really digging this water thing here. I'd like one in my house. Once I get a house, and that would of course be after I figure out where I'm going to live." She realized she was rambling and shut her mouth.

While Tuck ordered and picked the wine, she watched him. The man she was used to seeing was the opposite of the one before her, yet he wore both personas well.

"You're awfully quiet," he said. "Uncharacteristically so."

She tinkered with her napkin. "Not sure what to say that won't have me sounding like a loon."

"How about you tell me about work?" He must have noticed her hesitation for he amended the question. "How was your two weeks?"

This she was fine discussing. "It was absolutely wonderful. Great to see old friends and spend my days getting dirty instead of sitting behind a desk. Been thinking it may be in my best interest to get back in. Not sure yet." She drank some water and her attention was snagged again by the changing colors. "Have a fractured rib from a ballgame but—"

"You fractured a rib?" He leaned closer, concern present on his features. "And you're thinking about going back in the Marines?"

"Yes," she said airily. "I did it sliding into second." She grinned wryly. "But we won the game so it was worth it."

"And your rib now?"

"Will be sore for a while." She lifted her shoulder indolently. "Not a big deal. I'm not doing anything which will hurt it for a while."

His expression told her he wasn't on board with her cavalier attitude toward her injury. Then again, it could be about her going back into the Corps. He had a slight scowl on his face. Their order came and she thanked the man after he had placed it all down. The presentation was so nice on the plate, she wasn't sure she wanted to eat it—seemed like it should have its picture taken instead of being devoured.

He'd ordered her grilled Alaskan salmon, wild rice and steamed veggies. The fact he'd remembered how much she enjoyed salmon was touching. She lifted her wine glass and toasted him before sipping the liquid. Not typically a wine drinker, she was pleasantly surprised with the taste.

"What'd you get?" she asked him, staring at his plate.

Okay, so I wasn't paying attention to what he ordered for himself. I was busier staring at him after I told him what I'd like.

"Veal."

"Baby cow." She tsked. "Poor thing."

He cut and ate a bite. "It did its job well."

She laughed and turned her attention to her own plate, tasting her salmon. After putting her napkin on her lap, she cut some salmon and ate a few bites. It fell apart in her mouth. "Done to perfection." She tried a bit of everything else on her plate and found them in the same caliber, perfect.

Suddenly she was struck with a case of the nerves. With a deep breath, she stared at him. "I'm fucking nervous over here," she admitted with a shaky laugh.

He rested his elbows on the table and gave her his too-damn-sexy smile. His normal smile actually, which was one of the things that had first attracted her to him. The dimple was present and she had the oddest urge to lean closer and dip her tongue into it. Just see where that led them.

"Me too." He drank some wine. "I'm not sure why either of us are."

She began to relax. "Me either. I mean, I've seen you naked. Not sure why sitting here across from you is making me a bundle of nerves."

His brown eyes heated. "Dinner will be extremely short if you continue the discussion of our naked bodies."

Tingles shot out from her clit and spread throughout her body, tightening her nipples. The urge to slide all over the seat and moan was great, yet she refrained — with immense difficulty.

She gave a small shrug. "Just a comment."

Danger lurked in his gaze. "Like me merely commenting how I want to fuck you against the nearest wall and have those damn heels of yours digging into my back as you scream my name at the top of your lungs?" He pursed his lips. "True, it is just a comment."

She stared at his mouth as he ate another bite, her core temperature nearly through the roof. Licking her lips, she focused on her meal.

"How's work going for you?" she asked.

"Staying busy. The museum is coming along well, though. It would be faster if Schaffer would stay away. We can't trust the man to walk around alone so someone always has to be with him. And he comes all the time to *inspect* our progress."

She snorted. "He stopped by my office the other day. Wanted to ask me to another golf game. I mean, he did ask but he wanted me to go with him."

"And you said?"

There went his voice, dropping and getting all sexy deep again.

"I politely reminded him I don't date clients and I wouldn't be going out with him anyway. Oh, and how much I despised the game of golf. I think he got the picture by the time I was ranting about how much water it wastes just to keep the greens green. He left before I could get to how the country clubs were too damn exclusive."

Tuck chuckled. "Isn't the Marine Corps exclusive?"

She held his gaze. "Everyone has the chance to get in. There are some clubs I wouldn't even be allowed past the door because I don't have a dick. Or because of the color of my skin. The Marines aren't like that. If you can physically do it, you're given a shot to prove you have what it takes to be one of us."

"Think he'll be back to see you?"

"Doesn't matter. I told Connie to tell him I wasn't available if he showed up alone. If he comes with his father I'll talk. Otherwise, not there."

"Connie is wicked funny. I enjoyed hanging out with the two of you. So did Steve."

"She is that. A lot of people don't get to see that side of her."

"Sure is different than the woman behind the desk at your company."

She nodded. "Very much so. But she's one of the first friends I made when I moved out here. I just also tend to forget she's capable of being laid-back."

"Is it dangerous for her to work reception? I mean, the rest of you are behind that door but what if someone angry comes in?"

Her normal hesitation cropped up again and she dabbed the corners of her mouth. "We know who's arriving before they even get in the room. And she can more than take care of herself."

"She's such a little thing. How can she do that?"

"Connie can kick my ass before I even know what happened."

"No way."

"Yours and Steve's as well. Oh yeah, she's a multi-trained martial artist. I don't even know how many she knows or how many belts she has. Don't tell anyone that, however."

"I wouldn't—not that I'm believing it. She's like a little china doll."

She shook her finger. "Don't call her that. Not unless you don't want to continue standing upright for a week or so."

"Wow. Volatile woman with volatile friends." He winked.

"Me? I'm not."

"Right," he drawled out the word. "I believe that."

After their dessert, Tuck paid and they left to get back in his truck.

"Thank you for dinner."

"My pleasure. But we're not done yet."

Why did those five words send such a thrill through her?

* * * *

Tuck strolled along the River Walk with Ariel beside him. The weather was cooperating—off in the distance he could see some lightning but for the moment, they had a nice breeze as they meandered. Her arm was looped through his and her head rested upon his shoulder.

Many men stared at her as they passed—some women as well. He didn't blame them—she was killing him with her attire tonight. It had gone well, their first official date. At least he believed so. More were definitely in the plans.

"Sometimes I forget how nice the River Walk is," she said as they sidestepped some children running along the networked walkways. "I don't spend enough time exploring this city."

"What else did you want to see?"

"I've not even gone to SeaWorld yet. That's just crazy."

He made a mental note to take her there. "There are only so many hours in the day, Ariel. Give yourself some slack."

His mind drifted back to her comment about rejoining the Corps. That had created a big ball of sourness in his gut. He didn't want her to leave. At all. Hell, he was half in love with the woman and had been since they'd met. Most of the women he'd dated — slept with — prior to Ariel had been one-dimensional.

A fact he had wanted, because he knew there was nothing permanent about them. No need to worry about attachments and he could focus on getting his architectural firm up and running without having to think about if he was giving someone else enough attention. None of that had mattered when he first met Ariel.

In that moment, he'd known he'd be willing to do whatever it took in order to keep her happy and do what he had to for himself. But she'd not shown interest in him, so he was in the friend category. She didn't date much but it killed him whenever he saw her out with another man. And she'd never disparaged him for his dating habits — or man-whoring as Steve called it.

She fitted him. He fitted her. All he had to do was get her to see it as he did. One good thing to come from tonight was that he knew he could finish his plans and get them off to Richard finally. For the last bit he'd been missing to make his design perfect had come to him. It was now clear what he had to do.

"How about some ice cream?" he offered.

"After that dessert I ate?" She placed her hand over her belly. "Oh hell, sure. Why not. I'm walking it off."

They'd be working more of it off later if things went his way. He guided her to a table beneath a red umbrella and smoothed his hand along her cheek. "Be right back." He took a few steps away then looked back—she was watching him and even the approaching darkness couldn't hide the desire in her gaze.

"Same as you like at the ballpark?"

She gave him a thumbs-up and he went on his way to get her some. It didn't take him too long before he was on his way back. He paused before getting back to where she sat, taking a moment to watch her. She'd turned her attention to the San Antonio River and the boats that cruised up and down it.

He allowed his gaze to linger over the firm leg showing through the cut of her dress. Damn, he wanted her. Shoving his lust back, he closed the distance to her. "Here we go."

Her smile blinded him as she turned it on him. "Thank you." She smiled as she took the spoon and dipped it into her waffle cone cup full of chocolate ice cream.

He sat beside her and took a bite of his as well.

"What kind did you get?" she asked.

"A few flavors." He smirked. "Vanilla, chocolate, mint and strawberry."

"Such a kid, Tuck."

He took another bite. "Do you have plans this weekend or can I take you out again?"

She thought for a moment. "Sorry, not this weekend. I'm doing a—" She tipped her head and pointed her spoon at him. "You could come with me. If you liked."

He sucked some ice cream off the spoon. "I have *every* intention of coming with you again, Ariel." He hid his smirk when her pupils dilated. "What are you doing?"

"Clean-up and rebuilding a few things at one of the places Prometheus Protections sponsors. This one is a church."

"I'd love to go with you. Do I need to bring any materials?"

"Nope, they're supplying everything we need. They just needed bodies to help out."

"Sounds like a plan then. What time do we need to leave?"

"About five thirty. We want to get a good jump on the workload before it gets too hot."

"Understandable. It's a date."

Her smile was almost shy and he let it go, just enjoying the time they were having. After they'd finished the ice cream, they walked more and made it back to his truck as the first drops of rain began to fall.

They dashed through to the door once they reached the apartment building. She headed for the stairs but he drew her back close to him. "Take the elevator with me," he murmured in her ear.

"We both know what happened last time I was in there with you."

"You've not been drinking like that."

She acquiesced and he held her close as they rode up. Lord, he didn't want to let her go into her apartment but he didn't say a word after unlocking the door for her. She faced him and rose up on her toes to kiss his cheek.

"This was a date date, right?"

"Yes."

"Then I will bid you goodnight. Thank you for everything, I had a blast."

He cupped her upper arms and pulled her nearer. "Soon, Ariel, we'll be back in bed together."

She smoothed a hand over his chest. "I'm sure we will, but not tonight."

He nodded. "Because it's a date date."

"Our first one."

He smiled softly. "Does that mean you are willing to have more?"

"That's exactly what it means, Pierce Carter."

He kissed her softly on the lips. "Tuck. I'll always be Tuck to you. Sleep well, Ariel. Have lots of explicit dreams of me so we can act them out together, later on." He brushed his erection against her and she whimpered. His determination not to push wavered so he backed off. "Goodnight, beautiful."

He walked across the hall, opened his apartment then went inside with a final look at her over his shoulder. More of that damn insistence he run back to her and fuck her long and hard against the wall hit him.

Two hours later, after the clock had passed midnight, he heard thumping out in the hall. He opened the door and found Ariel pacing back and forth before her open apartment.

"Ariel? What are you doing?"

Lord, she still wore the dress she'd had on for their date.

She looked up and stalked to stand before him. "New day, new rules." She wrapped her arms around him and kissed him. Her tongue surged through his mouth and he met it with a low rumble.

Lifting her with one hand, he used his other to shut the door of his place and took her back to hers.

The moment they were inside her apartment, he whirled her so her back was against a wall, drew the door shut then shoved his workout pants down, freeing his thick erection.

"Ariel," he rasped. "Are you sure?" He didn't know how he'd be able to stop what he was doing but if she said no, he'd find some way to walk away.

She curved her hand around his head and drew him close. "Fuck me, Tuck. Just fuck me." Then she kissed him again.

He could taste the alcohol but it wasn't enough to stop him. Her words were coherent and he did as she'd said.

With a single stroke, he buried his cock deep within her pussy. She arched her back and cried out to the room. Bracing one hand against the wall, he thrust in and out of her tight pussy.

Chapter Seven

Ariel screamed again, her voice hitting a note she didn't even know she could reach. Dear Lord, this man just got better and better. This wasn't tender or soft. It was hard, fast and totally what she needed.

"Bed," he rumbled.

She brushed back some of her sweaty hair from her forehead and leaned back in for another kiss. "Your call. Ain't that big of a place. I'm fine with here, couch, floor. Hell, even the kitchen."

"We'll get there," he vowed, cupping her ass and walking toward her bedroom, kicking free of his pants on the way. Each step jarred his cock, which remained buried inside her.

She wound her arms around his neck and held on. Her dress had been shoved up over her ass and as they relocated, he took one hand and began playing with her clit.

"Aw, fuck!" More waves of pleasure crashed over her.

"I totally intend to."

He strummed her like an instrument. His calloused fingertips only increased the sensations. At her bed, he turned and sat so she straddled him. She couldn't hold still and rocked on his length, seeing his eyes darken as he pinched her clit.

"I really want you naked," he said. "But having you in that sexy-as-fuck dress with these shoes is one hell of a turn-on."

Reaching behind her with one hand, she undid the clasp that held up the halter top. It fell forward, exposing her bare breasts. "Better?" she questioned, rotating her hips as she searched for that one spot she needed him to hit.

His lips covered part of one breast instantly. "Oh yeah," he mumbled around the flesh in his mouth.

She quivered as his fingers mimicked what his tongue was doing to her nipple. Flicks, swirls, it didn't matter. They worked in tandem with one another and set her catapulting toward another fevered peak.

Pushing him back so he lay on the bed, she bent down and kissed him. Hungrily. How a man managed to taste so good she hadn't any clue but he pulled it off. He held her shoulders before sliding his hands down to the edge of the dress over her ass, where it was bunched.

Leaving his lips, she moved down, pressing kisses along her way. Over his pecs and scraping her teeth along his nipples as well, loving the shudder he gave as she did so. She sat back up and smoothed her hands along his torso.

"You're in incredible shape, Tuck."

Inside her pussy, his cock jumped and she rocked on him. He stared at her, his eyes dark with passion and need.

"Don't make me take back over, Ariel."

"In a rush?" she asked.

"Yes. I want to come deep inside you and watch your eyes roll back into your head as I do."

She tightened around him and began moving slowly on his shaft. "My turn to pick the speed."

The man growled but stayed put, allowing her to do all the work. Utilizing her hips to the best of her ability, Ariel found a rhythm she preferred. He hit all the right spots, yet she could control how fast she made it to another orgasm.

Watching him through slitted eyes, she noticed the strain on his face. He wanted to wrest control from her but was refraining. She raked her nails down his chest and ground down onto him before picking up her speed. Up and down she moved, readjusting so her shoes were flat on the bed as he lifted her up and down.

He took her hands and she used them to help her balance as she rode him. Tendons stood out on his neck and she knew he was close. He began countering her actions with his hips and soon, together, they both came in a fierce rush.

She collapsed on him with a grin on her face and sighed heavily. The man was still hard inside her and when he rolled them over, she held his gaze as he began to stroke into her again.

* * * *

She woke to a cry in the room and it took her a moment to realize it had poured from her throat. Tuck lay between her legs eating her pussy with a skill some men just never learned. His tongue flicked her clit as he worked three fingers deep inside her.

"Come again on my tongue," he commanded.

There was no way she could argue with him. She came instantly. He replaced his fingers with his tongue and took it all in. Her inner walls were sore and she trembled with each rasp he delivered.

Tuck kissed his way up her now naked body—when the dress and shoes had left her, she was a bit hazy on the details—until he shared her taste with her. He cupped the back of her head and put them nose to nose. Tuck kept most of his weight off her and she knew it was because he was still concerned about her fractured rib. Honestly, she didn't give a damn. For a night like this, she was willing to risk it.

"You're not running this time, Ariel."

With a slow blink, she shook her head. "I don't have the energy to run anywhere."

He rolled to the side and gathered her close. "Good. Can we sleep in?"

"Not too long. I have to get my run in before it's too hot."

"Okay, how about this. Three more hours then we run. Get all hot and sweaty then come back here and shower."

Fighting off her yawn, she relaxed against him. "Sounds like a plan." She didn't struggle anymore against the lure of Morpheus.

* * * *

When they woke for the run, she rolled from bed after a long, lingering kiss and watched with contentment as Tuck strolled naked to pick up his workout pants. She got her outfit on and turned to find him observing her with more hunger in his expression.

"No, Tuck. I have to run."

"What about your rib?"

"What about it? It's fractured, I can still do things."

His grin was pure sin. "And very well too. But won't running aggravate it?"

"As opposed to all the stuff we did last night?" She scratched her head. "No, I'll be fine." She gestured at him. "I'll wait for you to change into something else."

"Be right back." He slipped out and she waited until she heard the door to her apartment shut before she ventured forth.

Going to her computer, she linked up her iPod and uploaded her recently updated running songs. She was still seated there when Tuck came back.

"Whatcha doing?" he asked, closing the door behind him and moving to her side.

"Uploading my music."

"What does the great Ariel run to?" He sat beside her, gave her another kiss then stared at the screen.

"I like upbeat music but when I'm tired as I am today, I generally go back to running with cadences like we did in the Corps."

"Seriously? Like what?"

"Like this one that says, 'Listen to the rhythm of the tiny, tiny feet. Sounds like the Army in a full retreat.'"

Tuck burst out laughing. "Sounds like a good one."

"It is for us. I'm sure the Army's not a fan but we don't much care."

She stared at his shorts and tank top. *I'm so ready to forgo this and just get him back into bed.* Her lips twitched. *Or the kitchen, couch and floor. As he promised, we got there.*

"What are you smiling at?"

She pushed up from the desk and unhooked her iPod. "Nothing. Let's go." Ariel stopped. "Is my running with music going to be a problem for you?"

"Not at all. Mine is in my pocket."

"Awesome." Attaching hers to the armband holder, she watched him do the same. Then she secured her key and they went downstairs and stretched before setting off on their run.

Tired when she got back from the six mile trek, she enjoyed their shared shower. He had her come three times before he allowed himself to find release. Tuck had grabbed some clothes from his place before the shower and he put them on. Steve didn't join them for breakfast so it was just the two of them.

"This thing on the weekend," he began.

She looked up at him. "What about it?"

"Can I invite some of the men who aren't working?"

"If you want, definitely. More the merrier."

His eyes twinkled. "Is that for everything?"

"So long as it doesn't involve sex for me, mostly I'd say yes. I'm not into anything like that."

"Damn, so that threesome is out."

"Only if I'm one of those three. You can do what you want."

"We both know what I want is you, Ariel. Don't try to start pushing me away now."

The man knew her so well. She cleared her throat then said, "Just making a comment."

His grunt was one of doubt. "I'll see what I can do with the guys. Some have this weekend off and they may want to come help."

She finished her juice. "It would be wonderful."

He took his plate to the sink. "Do you need any help with clean-up?"

"I got it. Go."

Tuck stood behind her and tipped her head back so they could see one another. He kissed her until she was ready to melt into the chair. *Into? Hell, try through.*

"Thank you so much for the date, Ariel. And I'll see you tomorrow bright and early. Breakfast is on me."

"I feel I should be thanking you," she admitted. "See you then."

One more kiss then he went to the door where he paused and turned. He shook his head and muttered, "So damn beautiful." Then he was gone.

It didn't take much time to clean up before she was on the way to work herself. Connie was there. She took one look at Ariel, slipped from her chair and followed her down the hall to her office.

"Oh my God, you had your nasty way with him again. I can see it all over your face. What happened to it just being a date where this didn't happen?"

Ariel faced her friend and shrugged. "I failed that miserably."

Connie burst out laughing before managing to calm herself. "How miserably?"

"All night long and this morning kind of miserably."

"Was it worth it?"

"Hell yes!"

* * * *

Tuck stretched his back and looked around where he was working on the church. Three of the men on his crew had stopped by as well. He found Ariel—she was standing with a few children as they worked on scrubbing off the graffiti on the outside wall.

She looked entirely delectable. Her cargo pants rode low on her hips—hips he'd held as he fucked her not that long ago. The white tank top she had on allowed

98

him to see the muscles in her arms as she worked. She'd pulled her hair into pigtail braids and he realized he wanted to hold them as she screamed his name.

"Stop thinking about sex."

He found Jasper beside him. "What are you talking about?"

"Dude, you're at a church and the way you keep looking at Ms Greene, there, is going to get the minister after you as he straps you to a seat with a one-way ticket to hell. I don't think the children need to have a visual of what it is you'd like to do with her."

He shook his head. "I don't know what you're talking about."

"Right. You're probably sporting wood right now. All these women and children around—you need to get yourself under control."

"Don't you have something else to be doing?" he snapped, annoyed that the man had caught him daydreaming about Ariel.

"Doin' it, man, I'm doin' it. So do you and it's not staring at your new girlfriend."

His new girlfriend. That he liked. "Go be productive, Jasper."

The man laughed and walked away. Tuck willed his body back under some semblance of control. Once he'd managed that, he left the saw and strolled outside for a break. It didn't take him but a few steps to realize he was walking toward Ariel.

"How's it going?" he asked coming up behind her.

Ariel turned to face him, her grin wide. "We're doing great. You?"

"Not bad." He winked at her. "Taking a break."

"I see. Slacking."

The children took up her chant and he shook his head at her. He grinned, unable to hide his amusement—he loved watching her interactions with kids. She turned back to them and clapped her hands.

"Why don't you three go grab some drinks and take a break yourself?"

"Yay!" They scampered off and she watched them leave.

"Thanks again for helping out. Not to mention recruiting the others to come as well."

He crossed his arms. "No need to thank me. They were happy to help." His gaze moved over Jasper, Todd and finally Milton who'd brought along his entire family. The only one who wasn't helping was the eleven-month-old, who was currently sleeping in a playpen set up in the shade where his mom and dad both could keep an eye on him.

"Still, it was an extremely thoughtful gesture, one you didn't have to do." She dipped her brush back in the soapy water and attacked the last bit of tagging that defaced the building.

"Jasper says it's because of my girlfriend." He watched her close, wanting to see her reaction to his statement.

"You have one?" She never turned around.

"Yes. Don't you?"

"Women haven't ever done it for me, so that would be a definite no."

He was tempted to smack her on that firm ass. "Not what I meant."

"Not sure how I am supposed to take it. You asked me a question, which referred back to your comment of having a girlfriend. I said no. Very basic question and answer."

"Tuck!"

He turned to see Jasper waving at him, beckoning him over. Ariel snorted and said, "Break's over."

"You're enjoying this," he retorted.

She peered at him. "Yeah. I kinda am. Catch ya later."

He reached out and tugged on one braided pigtail. "Leave these in for later. I have plans. You're giving me one hell of a fantasy here."

She winked at him. "Awesome. Can't wait. You may want to clear it with your girlfriend first."

Her braid slid free as she moved back to the wall and attacked it again. With great reluctance, he left her there and returned to Jasper's side. "What?"

"Man, we're here to work, not pick up women."

"Speak for yourself." He slid his safety glasses on and, with Jasper's help, set up the four sheets he was slicing through at one time.

The roar of the motor and the smell of sawdust made him feel at home. This was what he loved doing. Even with wanting to get to more of the design side of this business, he knew he would always want to be hands-on, getting dirty.

They worked well together and it didn't take them long to put up the boards and go back for more. As he passed a window, he spied Ariel again. She was beside the man who'd introduced himself as Slater. On her other side was Connie. She made him chuckle – in her blue shirt and white bib overalls with the pant legs rolled up, she appeared more like one of the children running around than a woman who, according to Ariel, could kick his ass.

Ariel and Slater were laughing at something. Tuck paused, smiling at her expression. So obvious for all to know her emotions, she didn't hide behind a wall of seriousness. Ariel loved life and it showed.

"And we've lost him again," Jasper drawled from behind him.

"Shut up, man. You've not lost me. I stopped for like a second."

"Yeah, but like he pointed out, your eyes get all goo-goo when you look at her." Todd punched him in the shoulder. "Although, that little one beside her is pretty cute. Is she available?"

"I don't know. Go ask her."

Todd puffed out his chest. "I may do just that. But we still have work to do."

Snorting, Tuck returned to the stack of plywood they were putting up. He readjusted his tool belt then grabbed some more and got back to it. They were working on a shed behind the church. It had been set on fire so there was more work to be done on it than some of the other places. After they got the plywood up, they'd put on the siding.

It was afternoon when two kids ran over and called them to lunch. Ready for some sustenance, Tuck and his crew followed the duo to where a large grill was being manned by the minister of the church. A long table full of sides and condiments, as well as dessert, met his gaze and all three of them groaned happily.

After placing two burgers on his plate with macaroni salad, potato salad and more, Tuck found himself surrounded by some of the older boys who'd been recruited to come help. They talked, laughed and asked him lots of questions. Across the way, he spied Ariel eating with Connie and another woman from Prometheus Protections. She toasted him with her red plastic cup.

Some of the boys wanted to get into construction and he gave them his card, telling them to look him up when they were a bit older and he'd help them out.

Lunch was filling and fun but then it was time to work again.

They finished up around eight that night and he waved to his friends as they drove off, saying they'd see him tomorrow. Unhooking his tool belt, he strode to where Connie and Ariel stood. They were beside Ariel's Land Rover and a green sedan.

"I'll see you tomorrow, Connie," Ariel said.

"You got it. Night, Tuck." She gave him a nod then got behind the wheel and drove off.

"Ready to head out?" Ariel faced him.

"After you."

She opened the hatch and he placed his belt in the back before heading to the passenger side.

As they drove he cracked his neck. "I'll bring my truck tomorrow."

"Okay."

He had been expecting a bit more of an argument and slanted his gaze at her. "No problem with that?"

"Should I have one?"

"Not sure. I'm thinking maybe you should but I'm glad you don't."

She laughed. "More of those others you have been with, I'm assuming. I'm not totally confrontational, you know. You want to drive, I have no problem with it. I'm just stoked you aren't running away and feel like coming back again tomorrow."

"Why are you so surprised I'm not bailing?" He was genuinely interested in knowing.

"You do this every day. I can't imagine it's fun for you to do the same thing on your days off."

"I love construction work. Besides, how sucky would it be if I didn't want to help out a church in need? What kind of man would that make me?"

"Like a lot of others who don't feel it's their job to help."

"I'm nothing like other men, babe."

"No argument there, Tuck. Not a single one from me."

He smiled and leaned back. "Is Connie dating someone?" He paused for a moment then added, "Todd wants to know."

"Not that she's told me. I can ask her tomorrow if you'd like."

"If it comes up."

Ariel laughed. "Really? If it comes up? We're women, we talk about anything. I can make it come up."

"Ain't that the truth," he muttered.

"Mind out of the gutter, Tuck Carter."

He shrugged dismissively. "Just talking true."

At their building, he walked up with her and kissed her at her door before heading into his own place. Steve wasn't home and he found a note from the man stating he'd be gone for another week.

He showered and changed, after which he crossed to the other apartment on his floor. After knocking, he waited.

"Come on in, it's open."

He entered and found her seated on her couch, book in hand.

"I've been meaning to ask you something," he said, shutting the door behind him.

"Dinner is in the oven and will be ready in about a half-hour."

"Nice to know, but that's not the question."

"What is?" She closed her book.

"You work at a security firm. Were a Marine. How is it you're okay with leaving your door unlocked as you do?"

She laughed. "Honestly, I don't."

"You call out for us to enter and we can. Hell, sometimes we just come over and walk in."

"I know. But it's not that simple."

"Really?" Call him skeptical.

"I carry around a device that allows me to see who's at my door. I can activate or disengage the lock at the top and bottom of my door dependent on who's there."

He turned to look at her door. There were black squares on the top. "The landlord is okay with this?"

"He doesn't know. They look like nothing. It's from work—Slater let me take them and give them a trial run. Soundless and very strong. Even if someone were to try and kick the door in, those would help stop them. Now, I know the door is flimsy but it wouldn't bounce in like could happen with just the deadbolt."

"Where's the camera located?"

"That's above the door."

"More from Prometheus?"

"Absolutely. It's kind of smart tech. Your face and Steve's have been entered and recognized as welcome. So you truly wouldn't have to knock at all. You can come right on in, unless I specifically want to keep you out and either counter the auto approval or take you from the safe list."

"Is that what you have at Prometheus?"

"Partially."

He was impressed. Grinning at her, he made his way to where she sat on the couch and drew her near. "How long do we have until dinner is ready?"

She tossed her book onto the coffee table and wrapped her arms and legs around him. "Long enough."

Chapter Eight

Ariel opened the door with a squeal. "Roxi!"

The women embraced and laughed.

"Ariel, look at you. You're looking better, I think, than when I saw you at the wedding."

"You are positively glowing. Come in." Past her friend, she saw Sam standing there, patiently waiting. Silent as ever. The smile was still in place when she hugged him as well. "Hi, Sam."

"Ariel." His voice was deep and she totally got why it affected Roxi so. "Good to see you."

"And you as well. How was the honeymoon?" she asked, ushering Sam in.

"It was wonderful. But I told you that, it's been months."

And Roxi was right. It had been. She'd been swept back into work and, combined with spending any free time with Tuck, it had flown by. She got them something to drink and sat down in her overstuffed chair, watching them together on the sofa.

Roxi still wore earrings all along her ears. It had been the one thing she'd missed while being in the

Corps, Ariel knew. She loved wearing all her hodgepodge of earrings. With curves to die for, dark skin that shone with good health and coffee brown eyes that twinkled with humor, Roxi was the picture of happiness. Roxi had her long hair pinned up, even though they were in the latter part of summer and early autumn. This was Texas and it did get warm.

Ariel turned her attention to Sam. The man was just gorgeous, no bones about it. Broad shoulders and a lean waist, he was fit. He moved with the grace and aura of a man who had lived in dangerous situations for most of his life. Sam was somber—he didn't smile much or laugh a lot but he doted on Roxi, so that made up for it in Ariel's opinion. As long as he took care of her friend, she couldn't care less how much he talked.

Sam still wore his dark hair in that easily identifiable Marine high and tight style. His chiseled features made him appear harsher than he was, she knew that. It had been her misconception the first time they'd met. His eyes were a startling shade of sapphire blue. Roxi had told her that when she'd first seen them, they'd reminded her of the evening sky's deep blue with an exceptionally understated violet tinge. Personally, Ariel had to agree with her.

"So what are the two of you doing here?" she asked.

"Visiting my friend."

She narrowed her eyes. "Roxi?"

"I'm pregnant."

Ariel jumped up. "Oh my God!"

Her screech was echoed by Roxi's. They embraced again.

"How far along are you? Do we know if it's a boy or a girl? And why the hell don't you look fat?" She tipped her head to the side. "I saw that smile, Sam.

You can't fool me." She winked at him before turning her attention back to Roxi.

"Just started my second trimester." She rubbed her belly. "I am getting fat."

"Oh, don't make me kick your ass. You're pregnant and weigh less than me."

"You're taller."

"Was that supposed to make me feel better?"

"Yes." Roxi kissed her cheek. "Of course it was." She held up a finger. "I'll be right back. Bathroom?"

Ariel pointed her in the right direction and as Roxi scampered off, she faced Sam. "You know if you don't stand up and hug me, I'm going to straddle you on that couch." She placed a hand over her heart as he basically shot up. "I think I'm hurt, Sam."

He rolled his eyes and pulled her in for a hug.

Wrapping her arms around him, she whispered, "Congratulations, Daddy." She stepped back after kissing his cheek.

"Thank you." In the next second, all traces of ease vanished from his face and she knew the look. This was the warrior. "Ariel?"

She glanced over her shoulder in time to see Tuck enter. "It's okay, Sam. Neighbor."

He relaxed slightly yet remained standing. Tuck, who'd been smiling, drew up a bit at the sight of them together.

"Sorry, didn't mean to intrude."

It didn't take a genius to see the questions in Tuck's expression.

"You're not. Come on in, Tuck. I'd like you to meet Sam Hoch. Sam, this is Tuck Carter."

The men shook hands, all the while sizing each other up. She nearly rolled her eyes.

"Christ, Ariel. Can I just say that this being pregnant thing has its definite downside. I had a great lunch and just threw it… Oh, hello. And can I say hello in a way that makes you uncomfortable? Who is this gorgeous man, Ariel?"

Ariel snickered and turned it into a cough before looking at Roxi so she didn't just fall into heaps of laughter. "This is my neighbor, Tuck. Tuck, this is Roxi. The wedding I went to earlier this year. Meet the happy couple." She dipped her head briefly. "The happy, pregnant couple."

Roxi snorted and walked toward them. "Please, that man is not allowed to claim pregnancy. I'm the one who's going through all the changes." She stuck out her hand. "I'm Roxi. Sorry about that puking comment earlier. What can I say, but I'm blunt."

Tuck smiled. "No problem. Congratulations, and nice to meet you both. What brings you to Texas?" He slipped his arm around Ariel and she leaned against him.

Roxi lifted an eyebrow. "Wait a minute. You're sleeping with him?"

Sam cleared his throat.

"Sorry, another one of those things I should probably think about before I speak." In a stage whisper she added, "Nicely done, Ariel. Dude is fine!"

Sam cleared his throat again and Roxi blinked innocently.

"We came to see Ariel and ask her if she'd be the godmother to this child."

"Of course I will!" she cried, hugging her friend again. When they separated, Sam escorted Roxi to the couch and pressed her to the seat.

"I'm not an invalid, Sam."

"Indulge me."

She grinned cheekily. "I did — isn't that what got me into this situation of carrying your baby?"

Ariel rolled her eyes then went to the kitchen to get some crackers and cheese to munch on. Tuck followed her.

"She's a riot."

"Yes, she is. Roxi has a great sense of humor."

"He seems a bit uptight."

She glanced at her friends. Sam had his hand curved along Roxi's cheek and was saying something to her. "He's a Recon Marine. They tend to be a bit serious. Look at him, the way he looks at her. That kind of love I can see from here. And that's all I care about — he'll take care of her and protect her and their baby." Her smile was wry. "Sam's a good guy. Had a hard life and once you know him more, he will relax."

"Do you want me to leave?" Tuck asked as he lifted the tray. "So you can spend some time with your friends?"

"No, you're more than welcome to stay. Totally your decision, though."

"I'm intrigued about you, Ariel, and I think Roxi may be able to enlighten me on some things."

"Shit," she muttered, following him back to the living room. "Was there anything special you wanted, Roxi? Fruit or anything else?"

She shook her head. "This is perfect, thank you."

Ariel took a seat across from Tuck, who gave her a wicked grin. This could prove to be disastrous for her. The one thing she didn't need to happen was for Tuck to get blackmail material on her.

"So," she said. "This godmother thing. What do I get to do? Spoil them rotten and be like the favorite aunt?"

"Something like that. Of course, if something happens to us, then the raising of said young'un will fall on you."

She didn't even hesitate. "I'm honored you'd choose me for such a thing."

"I know it's a lot to ask," Roxi said, "but I can't think —"

"Not a lot to ask, Roxi. Can I ask a question, though? What about Lalia?"

"Love her to death but she's not in a place right now where it would make sense for me to ask her this. I know how you are in a crisis situation and let's be honest, Lalia's not the best in them."

"I'm in," she said.

Roxi's smile said it all. They shared a look and a nod. The moment was shattered by Tuck.

"Tell me one of the most entertaining things you remember of Ariel from when she was a Marine."

"No, no, that's not necessary." Ariel glared at him and he only watched her with an innocent look.

"I think it is," Tuck inserted.

"Let me think."

"Seriously, Rox? You gonna throw me under the bus like that?"

"Of course. Why would you even ask me that? You know I will in a heartbeat. Now hush, pregnant woman thinking."

She grunted, rolled her eyes and stared at Sam. "I blame you for this, creating a monster."

"I know," he replied, nodding somberly.

"I also just want you to know I see that smile in those eyes of yours."

He nodded again. "I know."

"Oh," Roxi said. "How about the time we were at the movies and I was complaining about being hungry." She looked at Ariel. "Remember that?"

Yes, she did. "Evil bitch."

Roxi flipped her off. "Anyway. I was starving. We went there after getting done for the day and had finished a fifteen click run right before it. Had we stopped for food we would have missed the movie. So there we are, watching"—she pursed her lips—"some action, blow 'em up kind of movie, not recalling which one, and she finally gets fed up with me griping. We had no money for anything from the snack bar. So she reaches into her purse and smacks me with a packet, says, 'Here, eat this and stop your incessant whining.'"

"It was incessant. Lord, you were annoying. I was enjoying watching the destruction and there you were, every minute. 'I'm hungry. Waa. I'm hungry.' It was annoying."

"Again, Tuck asked me, not you, so zip it."

Ariel crossed her arms and muttered unpleasant things under her breath.

"I heard that," Roxi said.

"You were supposed to," she said in a sing-song voice.

"Whatever, whore. So, I look down to see what it was and she'd given me an MRE."

"What! You were hungry, I gave you some food." She threw her hands up in frustration.

Tuck and Sam were smiling and laughing.

"You gave me beef ravioli. Who the hell walks around with that in their pants pocket, really?"

She tried not to laugh as she recalled Roxi's expression. "The other one was Jamaican pork chop and noodles, I think. Or cheese tortellini."

Roxi waved a hand. "So there I am in the movie theater while people around me are eating popcorn, nachos and other things. Hot pretzels, nachos, hell, even pizza. But not me, I'm finger-eating a cold MRE."

"Evil heifer," Ariel said affectionately.

"Do you still carry them around with you?"

Adopting a superior expression, Ariel sniffed. "Not in my pocket, thank you very much."

"What about your vehicle?"

"It never hurts to be prepared," she said, her voice rising.

Roxi gave her a pointed look. "And you do it so well."

"Oh, this is good," Tuck said. "Tell me more."

"Well, there's the time with the condoms."

Ariel wiped her eyes as she howled with laughter. "He *so* doesn't need to know about that."

Roxi shrugged shamelessly. "I think he just may."

Tuck, curse him, agreed with Roxi immediately.

Slumping back in her chair, Ariel knew she was defeated. She crossed her arms and pouted. Roxi ignored her and did what she was always good at doing—told stories.

* * * *

Tuck tossed his gear in the back of his truck and walked for the office. The past week had been a blast. Ariel's friends, Sam and Roxi, had been around the entire time. They'd gone out, stayed in and all around had fun. The stories the women told on one another were just hilarious. It had been a long time since he'd laughed that hard. Probably since he and Steve had been with Ariel and Connie the night they'd lost power in the building.

The Hochs had left today and honestly, he was going to miss them. Sam had grown on him and he saw now what Ariel had pointed out to him that first time he saw the man. He was stoic but there was no denying his love for Roxi or their unborn son. The man didn't mind getting her food or waiting on her hand and foot — not that she let him, but Tuck knew he would have no issue doing it — and doing things a lot of men would deem unmanly. None of it bothered Sam.

He even felt bad for his initial jealousy toward him when he'd first spied him in Ariel's apartment. But walking in to find her practically in another man's arms hadn't sat well with him. Now that he knew, he was good with their relationship. Ariel hadn't asked him if he was, and he hadn't said anything to her about it. He was just better in his mind. No jealousy there. And he'd made a new friend.

Tuck had found Sam to be even more close-lipped about what he did in the Corps. The man's patented response had been 'I'm Recon,' — as if that was supposed to tell him what he did. Tuck had since looked it up on the Marines' website and had gotten more than Sam had said. He was impressed from the small bit he'd read and understood.

One day, he'd questioned Sam as to whether he would ever get out of the Marines. Sam had stood there for a moment, staring out over the River Walk — which Roxi had wanted to come down and see — and said, "I'd die in my uniform if I could. I'll serve until I can no longer do what I love to do so much with the accuracy I can do it with now. Once you have the desire to serve, it's hard to turn it off. Roxi got out because it was what was best for her nephew. But I know, daily, she misses it."

Tuck hadn't been sure how to respond to that. He was worried, the way Ariel talked about getting back in. He didn't want her to leave. Nor did he want her in danger.

He shook his head and pulled himself from the past with the Hochs and Ariel, where they had been like two couples double dating all the time. Ariel hadn't minded that he'd hung out with them.

Richard stepped out as Tuck neared the mobile building and Tuck gave the man a nod accompanied by a slight smile.

"Got a moment, Pierce?" Richard's hand was curved around the handle of a cane.

He frowned — when had the man needed assistance getting around? "Sure. What's up?"

"I need to set up a time for you to meet with me at the office building downtown. Do you have your schedule handy?"

He pulled out his phone and brought it up. "What were you thinking?"

"Sooner the better. I know things here are running smoothly but I'm not sure what else you have on your workload."

"My afternoon is clear if you'd like me to stop by after I finish work here."

He dropped his gaze back to the hand on the top of the cane and watched his fingers clench it repeatedly, as if he wasn't able to get a comfortable grip and needed it desperately. Tuck stood ready just in case he was needed. It bothered him to see Richard not feeling well.

"Say about four thirty?"

"I'll be there."

"Good lad. Good lad." Richard, it appeared to Tuck, spoke almost to himself. His friend and mentor walked to the waiting car and slid into the back after the driver opened the door for him.

Tuck remained in his current position until the black car pulled from the construction site. Running a hand down his face, he sighed heavily. Something was off with Richard. Unable to worry about that now, he went into the white building and relished the air conditioning blaring through the small space.

"Sherry," he said as he closed the door behind him.

"Hey, Tuck. What can I get for you?"

He looked at her—one of the two women who worked with their crew. She was tough. Before she'd fallen off some scaffolding and had material crush her leg, Sherry had been out there with them. She walked with a noticeable limp now but none of the men gave her a hard time. Not in the same way they might if she'd been some empty-headed, big-breasted girl. Sherry had a steel trap for a mind and if she caught anyone staring at her breasts, she might take their cock, just on principle. She could—and did—put up with healthy doses of teasing, but if a new worker got out of hand, Sherry had no problem putting them in their place.

"Need some blueprints on the back part of the museum. It looks different than I thought it would in my head."

Normally he would have those outside with him but it had been raining off and on and he'd needed to be outdoors to look, so the papers were all in the office.

"Richard was looking at them a moment ago. Since I haven't had time to put them away, they're on the table to your left." She came from the small kitchen holding a cup of coffee and sipped from it.

He moved there and saw she was spot on. "Thanks. What was Richard doing here?"

"Beats me, Tuck. I don't question the boss man."

"Bullshit," he said laughing. Tuck gazed over at her and saw the grin on her face as well. "Did he seem as if something were bothering him? Not work related, but physically?"

She moved toward him. "Physically? What's going on?" All joviality vanished. Sherry was nothing but business and concern.

"I saw him outside and I've never seen him with a cane before. Not to mention he couldn't seem to get a good grip on it. He looked off balance to me and I just wanted to know if you'd seen it as well."

She shook her head. "Nope. But to be honest, I didn't see the cane either. He was sitting at the table looking over them when I walked in. When it was time for him to leave I was in the back. I mean, he was there when I went to the back to fix my coffee and you were there when I returned."

He shrugged. "Okay, thanks."

"Think something is up with him?"

"I do but I'm not sure what it is." He placed his elbows on the table and rested his chin on laced fingers. "I'll figure it out."

She put her hand on his shoulder. "Let me know if there's anything I can do."

"Will do, thanks."

She went back to her desk and got busy doing orders and the numerous other things she did there. He found what he needed and saw what the dimensions of the back room were supposed to be.

"No way that's what it truly is." He jotted the numbers down on a sheet of paper then shoved it in his pocket before rolling the blueprints up and returning them to their proper place. "See you, Sherry."

"Bye, handsome," she called out without looking up from the computer. "Thanks for putting them back."

"Anything for you, babe."

"I'll keep that in mind."

He chuckled as he stepped back outside. More rain fell and he hunched his shoulders as he walked back to the museum. Once he stepped inside, he shook the water from his hair and withdrew his cell phone.

"Calling me at work now, Tuck?" Ariel's question was both teasing and welcoming.

He smiled and strode to the back. "Hey, beautiful. Are you busy?"

"Well, I'm at work. Aren't you?"

"Yes, but that's why I am calling you. Do you have time to come down here?"

"Everything okay?"

"It would be easier for me to ask with you standing here."

"I can leave in five."

"Drive carefully, it's raining."

Her laughter warmed him. "You know they did give me a window in this box of an office. I've been watching it. After the heat from most of the summer, I'm pleased to see this rain."

"Just get here, woman."

"Snapping a salute here. See you in a few."

Ending the call, he did another scan of the room. It just didn't seem right. He made his way slowly back to the front and waited for Ariel. When she arrived, he watched her get out of her LR3.

Today's suit was black, pants rather than skirt, and did nothing to quell his imagination of what he knew very well lay beneath the material. Sure strides brought her across the muddy ground and if it bothered her, she didn't show it.

"What's up?" she asked, shaking the water off her umbrella.

"No 'hi, honey, how are you?'"

"Nope. What's up?" She leaned the dripping blue item against the wall.

He saw she had her clipboard binder with her. Reaching to the left, he grabbed a hard hat and placed it on her head.

"Really? This again?"

"It's a construction site, babe."

Her grumbles made him smile. "Fine. What did you need me to see?"

He began walking and she fell into step with him. "It's in the back, one of the rooms there. I needed you to look at it and tell me if the equipment y'all use is there and if so, would it take up the room it is appearing to do so."

In his periphery, he saw her frown. She opened her clipboard and pulled out a sheet of paper—a shrunken down version of his blueprints. Her expression was serious as she navigated the walk and stared at what she held.

He showed her into the room and immediately she shook her head. Tuck took off his hard hat and shoved a hand through his hair before putting it back on.

"No. This isn't the room we have our things. Our stuff that we added is in the electrical room. The dimensions are all off in here, though."

He crossed his arms and watched as she circulated the room. She stopped on the other side and pointed at the wall.

"Here."

Tuck went to her side. "Here what?"

"I'd say this is a panic room. It opens here."

"How do you know this?" He worked construction for Christ's sake and he couldn't tell.

"I've done this for a while. It's the best place in the room to have one. Look at the ceiling — that little divot in there is a sensor. I'd bet dollars to doughnuts there's another one up on the second floor." She cleared her throat. "And in the basement."

"Who the fuck's been messing with my construction site?" He was furious. "Let's go check upstairs."

"Sure."

"Wait. Can you open this?"

"I could. Did you want me to?"

"Not yet. Let's go see if there's one upstairs as well."

She shrugged easily. "Your call."

It might be but he was getting pissed. They headed for the stairs and Tuck tried to figure out what the hell was going on.

* * * *

"Care to tell me why there are panic rooms in the museum?"

Richard blinked slowly at him from where he sat behind the large teak desk. "What are you talking about?"

"You had to know, Richard," he said unwilling to play the game where one person pretends not to know what another is talking about. Tuck especially wasn't willing to do it with this man. "You've had other people there at night. Is that when it was put in?" He pursed his lips. "They, they were put in?"

Once Ariel had left, Tuck had come to Richard's office.

"How did you figure it out?"

Guess that was confirmation, somehow. "Blueprints." He stepped closer to the desk and sat in the chair after dragging it up. "I know this is your company, but it's partly my name as the foreman on the project. Why wasn't this on the original blueprint?"

"Hear me out, Pierce. Will you tell me how you figured it out? What prompted you to go back to the blueprints?"

"Why wouldn't I go to them? I want everything to be perfect. The size of the room appeared off to me so I went to check. Then I called Prometheus Protections and had Ms Greene come meet me. While she was there I asked her if her men could have stored some equipment there. She looked around the room and found the entrance then told me there were probably ones on the other floors as well. We looked and discovered she was right. So she opened them."

Richard sat forward. "She opened them?"

"I told her to, it wasn't her idea." Immediately the need to protect Ariel hit him.

"I thought you were kidding when you said she'd found the entrance."

"Why would I joke about that? This is serious, Richard."

"Listen to me, son. The owner, Gerald, came to me after the plans had been agreed upon. He asked me if they could be added in. He's paying good money to do it and didn't want the rooms a matter of public record.

Tuck scowled. "So you had other workers go in after we finished the rooms and change them.

"Yes."

There was so much he could say but he kept it contained. It wasn't his company so he truly had no say in the matter. "Whatever. What did you need to see me about?"

"Your architectural firm."

"I'm not sure I'm starting one." Tuck rose. "Besides why would you help me? It's obvious you don't trust me since you kept me out of the loop on that whole panic room thing." Yes, he knew he sounded bitter but damn it all, he was. "You've known me for a long time, Richard, and I thought you trusted me. Guess I was wrong."

Tuck left, ignoring the man's calls to come back in. He slammed his hands on the steering wheel before he drove home.

Chapter Nine

Ariel stared at the phone she'd just hung up. It seemed odd to have heard the words she had just been told. Pushing to her feet, she looked around her living room. "Not really sure why I'm paying for a place when it seems like I'm never here to enjoy it."

She went to her bedroom and sat on the edge of the mattress before flopping back. Eyes closed, she tried to imagine this working. She heard the click of her front door and knew within moments she'd have company, yet remained where she was.

"Babe?"

"Back here."

Tuck sat beside her. She cursed her body's immediate and apparent instinctive response to his scent. One powerful thigh pressed up against her and she cracked open her eyes.

"Get it all figured out with your boss?" she asked.

"Oh yeah. He had some other men go in and add the rooms. They didn't want them on the blueprints." He scoffed. "I don't know why I feel betrayed."

Tuck dropped back to lie beside her and she lowered her lids again.

"Sorry."

"Shit happens. How was your day?"

She made a face. "Well, I'm going to leave for a while."

He shifted on the mattress. "What?" There was disbelief in his tone.

"I have been assigned a personal protection gig."

"Could you look at me, please?" His voice was all deep and terse.

She turned her head and opened her eyes. "Better?"

He drew a breath and expelled it heavily. "Not really. What is this about a personal protection thing? I thought you didn't do that."

She read the frustration in him, exceptionally visible with his clenched jaw.

"*Normally* I don't. I prefer to be elsewhere in the company but I can do it and I'm damn good at it if I do. Slater thought I would be perfect for the job and apparently the client agreed." She stared at the ceiling. "I leave in two days."

"For how long?"

"I don't know." She shifted and brought her feet up to rest on the bed as well.

"Where?" It was as if she could hear the frown in his voice even though she'd since stopped looking at him.

"Can't say."

"Who are you guarding?"

She didn't so much as move. "Can't tell you that either."

"Damn it, Ariel. What *can* you tell me?" He pounded a fist on the bed.

She tensed. "That I leave in two days and don't raise your voice at me."

"I'm not." He cleared his throat and began again in a lower, more even tone. "I'm not."

"I just got the call literally three minutes before you came in the door, Tuck. I'm still trying to digest this myself."

"What did Slater tell you?"

She propped herself up on her elbows and turned her watchful stare to him. He'd sat up and was staring down at her, anger and uncertainty in his gaze. "I told you what I could of what he said to me."

"Bullshit."

She raised an eyebrow. "Excuse me?"

"You can tell me more."

"No I can't. Personal protection isn't something you go blabbing about, Tuck. Surely you know that." She made a face. "Or can at least understand if not appreciate it."

"Who am I going to tell? I'm your boyfriend, for fuck's sake. Why can't you tell me?"

"Aside from the fact I'm not supposed to?"

"Yes!"

She stood and put fisted hands on her hips. "I was trying to spare your feelings."

His brown eyes grew wide. "My feelings? Why would you need to spare them?"

"Because I'm going in as someone's fiancée."

Every inch of him went rigid. Tuck swallowed and said in a voice that, in her opinion, was *way* too controlled, "What did you say?"

"You heard me. I'm going in as the man's bride-to-be."

"What man?" Irritation laced his tone.

She shook her head. "Tuck, you know I—"

"What man, Ariel? What? Man?" His question was more an animalistic growl than actual words.

"Congressman Dovers' son. He's coming back home and they want him to have some protection."

When Tuck pushed to his feet and moved toward her, every step screamed predatory and dangerous. "So you're going to be kissing him and sleeping with him."

"I'm *going* to be doing my job."

His smile wasn't pleasant. "I'm sure."

Anger sparked within her as well. "Listen to me, I wasn't looking to do this. I didn't go ask to be slated as his fiancée. It was assigned to me because they thought I was the best fit. I may have to kiss him, yes. But I won't be sleeping with him." *I've never met the man before.*

"Yet you weren't going to tell me that."

"I was trying to protect you!" she hollered.

"Moving up in the world, aren't you?" he sneered. "Going from dating some no-name construction worker to being engaged to a congressman's son." He shook his head. "I didn't need your protection, Ariel. I just needed you to think me worthy of telling me the truth." He walked to her bedroom door. "Have fun."

"Tuck!" she called out.

He stiffened but didn't stop, just continued on his way.

"Damn it!" she cried out after the door to her apartment shut. She warred with the notion of going after him and not.

It took her no more than a minute to make up her mind and she stomped to the door before going across the hall and letting herself in. Tuck stood in the kitchen, popping the top off a beer. His gaze was cold when he looked at her.

She kicked the door shut behind her and made a beeline to the man who was driving her absolutely crazy, in both a good way and a bad. Keeping the counter between them—she wasn't sure her hands wouldn't be around his neck otherwise—she glared up at him, matching him glower for glower.

He still clenched his jaw, as he'd been doing at her place, and she watched the play of muscles in his arm. *Damn, can I not think about sex around him?* Apparently not even anger could stop her desire for this man. But it was something she could control.

"How dare you!" she seethed.

He raised a brow and drank from his beer. "Problem?" His word was crisp and bitten off.

"Yes. I told you what I could. I shouldn't have told you what I did and I broke that rule. Then you dare to try and be righteous about what I may or may not have to do." She dragged her fingertips across the smooth countertop as if she had claws and could tear through the material.

"So I'm supposed to be okay with my girlfriend kissing, or fucking, another man?" His grin was tight and definitely didn't reach his eyes. "I don't think so, babe. I'm not that kind of man." He drank some more. "I never will be."

"I do what's necessary for the job."

"Must be nice to have a built-in excuse for cheating."

She went ramrod straight, eyes narrowing. "Excuse me? A built-in excuse for cheating?"

"That's what it is when you're in a committed relationship and sleep with another."

She longed to punch him. "Don't worry, it's not a concern any longer."

It was his eyes that narrowed this time. "How so?" He crossed his powerful arms, beer dangling from one hand.

"Because" — she whirled around to head for the door and jerked it open — "I no longer have a boyfriend." She exited and slammed the door behind her. "Arrogant bastard."

Back in her apartment, she went to her closet and withdrew a suitcase. Flopping it on her bed, she stared at her dresser and thought about the clothing she needed to pack. She shook she was so furious. *How dare he! How fucking dare he.*

It's not like I asked for this and I never said I would be sleeping with anyone. She'd never met the man before — it wasn't like she was about to fall into bed with him.

* * * *

She didn't see Tuck again until the day of her departure. She'd set it up with Steve to get her mail and water the few plants she had. Tuck was leaving his apartment at the same time. His gaze singed as she stood there, hand on her suitcase handle.

With a blink, she started to walk toward the stairs, ignoring both her desire to talk and kiss him.

"Not even going to say goodbye?"

"Hello, Tuck." She started down the stairs. "Goodbye, Tuck."

Of course he wouldn't leave her alone. Instead of taking the elevator, he began down with her. When he reached for the handle she glanced at him.

"What are you doing?"

His gaze didn't give anything away. "Trying to carry your bag, if you'd release your hold on it."

She stopped on the landing, released the bag and tapped her foot. After rubbing her forehead, she turned her left earring.

"What possible reason — "

His mouth landed on hers with a ferocity that stunned her. Backed into the corner, she could only hold on as he dominated her. He swept through her mouth with angry strokes. Her pussy creamed and she held onto him as if it were the only thing ensuring she wouldn't crumble boneless to the ground. And it very well may have been the only thing holding her up.

It seemed the kiss ended before it had even truly begun. He stepped away from her and hefted her suitcase as if it weighed nothing—for him, it probably didn't—and continued down the steps.

He was out of sight by the time she regrouped and she hastened after him. *Damn!* Tuck walked right out to her vehicle then gave her a look she understood to mean *unlock the SUV.* So she did.

He placed her items in the back then went to hold the driver's door for her. Thoughts completely jumbled, she allowed him to assist her into the vehicle.

"Stay safe," he murmured, brushing the back of his hand along her cheek.

He desired to kiss her—she could read it in his gaze—and part of her willed him to follow through. Unfortunately, he didn't. Instead he backed away and closed the door on her.

"I have no idea what just happened there," she said with a huff of air.

She could see him striding away in her rear-view. There were no look-backs nor any hesitation from him. However, she didn't leave her parking spot until that fine denim-swathed ass disappeared from sight.

* * * *

Tuck sat at a conference table waiting to be joined by Richard, who had requested his presence. Helen, his secretary, had told Tuck to sit tight here. So here he waited, taking in the opulence of the conference room. From the sleek mahogany table, zero gravity chairs and the artwork on the walls that cost more than a month's rent for him, the room screamed wealth.

The door opened and in came Richard, a file in one hand and his cane in the other. He slid it along the gleaming top. Tuck stopped it with his fingers.

"What's this?" he asked.

He was aware his response was a bit on the sharp side, but he was still put out by being kept in the dark about the panic rooms.

"Read it."

Richard sat at the head of the long table, nearly all the chairs between them. Tuck flipped the file open. A contract lay there. He read it.

Holy shit.

"Is this a joke?" he demanded of the man across the room from him.

"Surely you know me better than that by now, Pierce. Why would I go through the trouble of drafting a contract merely if it's nothing more than a joke? I have more important things to do with my time."

The reprimand was there but Tuck ignored it. He glanced from the paper to his mentor again. Richard's cane rested on the table and he'd leaned back in the chair, eyes closed. Didn't look like a man pressed for time to get something else accomplished — more like one about ready to take a nap.

"You're fronting me the full amount to start my own architectural business. As well as a construction one." He peered at Richard again. No change in him. "And you're only stipulation for being paid back is 'when it won't bother me to do so?' Richard, this is insane."

"I can do whatever I want with my money, Pierce. I've earned it therefore I can spend it however I want."

"You can, but this is bordering on lunacy."

One eye opened and the force of the glare slammed him. "So you don't want your own company?"

Tuck scoffed. "Of course I do."

"Okay then, what's the problem? I want to give you the money and you could definitely use it."

"And your children? How will they feel about this?"

He gave a dry bark of amusement. "Not that I give a damn what they think. They didn't earn any of this. Not to mention," he said, sitting up. "What I'm giving you is less than what they've blown on frivolous crap like cars and other things. Mind you" — he rapped his knuckles on the table — "that's each of them alone. Remember, I have five kids."

Tuck knew there was strained tension between them all but he'd not known it was that bad. "What's this about the land?"

"That property we saw a while back. It and one hundred acres are for you to build that house. I especially like the water wall you added to the master bedroom. Nice touch."

Tuck smiled. That had been put in after he and Ariel had been on their first date.

"It's still too much —"

"Let me put it to you this way. You accept it now or when I die I'm leaving my entire empire to you." He drummed his fingertips this time. "I may do that anyway — give me a final chuckle and show my leech kids they aren't in any way getting what their whore of a mother couldn't get from me. Pre-nup, son. That's the only reason I still have what I have."

Tuck reclined and swirled toward Richard. "I get it. It's your money."

"Damn straight. And I'll do whatever I want with it."

"Right. I still think it's insane."

Richard leaned forward. "Humor me. Or can you sit there and tell me you're not the least bit interesting in signing a sheet of paper that will get you the money."

"Of course I am, it's everything I've wanted. I'm trying to protect your interests here."

"Don't worry about me, son. Are you trying to tell me you're not worth the investment? That you'll fuck it all up and drink away the money?"

He frowned. "No, of course not."

"Then let me bank roll it for you. Sign the paper. There's a pen there."

He wanted to so badly but couldn't muster the strength to lift the gold plated pen that had been attached to the file.

"I don't want to take advantage of our friendship."

"Come down here. Don't make the old man get up." He beckoned. "And bring that file."

Tuck did as ordered and lowered himself into the seat to Richard's right.

"I think of you as a son, Tuck."

He started at the use of his nickname. In the many years they'd known one another, the man had never — not even once — called him Tuck.

"And one I'm proud of, unlike the other wastrels. I want to do this for you. I don't even need a contract, we can go to the bank now, you present your business plan and I will transfer funds to an account for you to use. No interest charged." Richard moved his cane to the left. "Listen to me. You see this as a risk. I see it as an investment. I give grants and loans to people all the time to start up their own businesses. Only, however, when I believe in them. Why do you think I've been pushing you to finish the house plans and your business plans for your firm and company? I'll tell you—because I believe in you. You, Pierce, and your ability to turn into a huge success. You are already building a following—the companies we work with love having you on the job and some have even really gone for the changes you've suggested in the blueprints of either homes or businesses. It's time for you to stop working for me and get out on your own."

Tuck blinked and stared at his friend and mentor, baffled.

Richard laughed. "I'm not losing my marbles. I want to make this happen. Three days from now, we'll go to the bank and get you the money. First, however, since you seem to want to not believe in my trust for you, you'll stand here in this room and present your business plan to me and a few others whom I'll bring in. Deal? Good." Richard got to his feet. "Let's get some food."

This was truly happening. Tuck couldn't believe it but as he walked with Richard to the elevator, not even his disbelief could wipe the smile from his face. He couldn't wait to tell Ariel.

Chapter Ten

Ariel sipped from the flute of champagne she held. In truth, she merely let a few drops in, her goal to give the impression she was drinking. This was the fourth party in a week and she was reaching the end of her goodwill. It wasn't her style to get all gussied up and stand around talking about others who don't have as much.

"How's my beautiful lady?"

Jackson Dovers slid his arm around her and placed a kiss on her cheek. She was one lucky woman—the man looked a lot like Tyrese Gibson and had this way of making her think things she shouldn't. They had a good rapport with one another and she wanted to keep it that way.

"Are you ready to leave?" she asked. She brushed her gaze over him, taking in the way he wore his tuxedo. The man was downright handsome, no denying that fact. At the last minute they had nixed the fiancée thing for her. She said if she was only there temporarily, it didn't make sense. If he was supposed to be a playboy then there was nothing wrong with her being there for a short time then gone from the picture.

A few people drifted near as was customary when he stopped long enough. He was big news and everyone, women especially, wanted to find out how and what he'd been doing. It didn't matter that she was supposed to be his girlfriend—it surely didn't stop them from making advances. Both married and unmarried.

"Leave all this to spend some quality alone time with you? Baby," he said with a wink for the crowd, "we could have stayed home and done more, um, pleasurable things." He nuzzled her neck. "Although seeing you in this dress was well worth it. Sapphire chiffon looks stunning on you. And sexy. Can't wait to unwrap you."

She knew she looked good—the iridescent layered chiffon dress was a perfect fit. The sweetheart bodice tempted, it was sleeveless and the asymmetric hem added to the entire package. The fitted bodice had pleating diffusing from the side seam and although the hem reached the floor, there was a side slit that allowed a peak of leg to sneak through when she walked. Silver heels rounded out the image.

Ariel could see envy on some of the women's faces. With a smile, she placed the flute on a passing waiter's tray. "Let's go then."

He cupped the nape of her neck and rubbed. "If y'all will excuse us."

From her periphery, she spied a man watching them, gaze hard. To most people he would have merely been watching the couple but for Ariel, there was something else going on. She racked her brain and realized why he seemed familiar.

"Who's that man to my left?" she asked him before stopping and turning in the direction.

A ripple went through Jackson before he shrugged with forced nonchalance. "No clue." He tightened his hold on her. "Let's get the car."

It was waiting for them as they departed the large mansion and walked into the Texas night. Fall had arrived and it was finally a bit cooler. The valet held her door for her as she slipped into the passenger seat of his glossy red Ferrari 458 Spider hard-top convertible. The top was up tonight. However, there'd been times when it had been down for some of their day trips.

As he got behind the wheel, she spied that same man on the top of the steps. Eyes narrowing, she decided to hold her tongue until they got back to his place. A relatively short drive to begin with. She'd found that when people had cars that could do nearly two hundred miles per hour, they tended to speed a bit.

Jackson slowed when he pulled up to the gate surrounding the congressman's home. He entered a code and the gate swung open only to shut after they had passed.

"Let me out here," she said.

"What?"

"Just do it and park your car. Meet me in the kitchen in a few, we need to chat." She climbed out and shut the door behind her. After he drove on, she made her way back to the gate and waited, hidden by the tall privacy shrubbery planted all around.

About five minutes later, another vehicle drove up where it slowed at the gate — a crotch rocket. The man idled the bike before he eventually continued on his way. Deep in her gut, she knew it was the same man from the party who'd been watching them so intently.

A light hum had her turning around. Security was riding up on a golf cart. The driver was Samuel—he'd been a security guard most of his adult life and was the head of it here. He knew what she was truly there for.

"What are you doing out here, Ms Greene?" he asked, stopping beside her and glancing about. He whistled. "Look at you in that dress. Get in here, I'll not have you walking back to the house."

She sat on the seat beside him. "Thanks. I need to know if you have any footage of a motorcycle hanging around. Crotch rocket, darker color. Just happened now and if that same make and model has passed by earlier."

"I'll look into personally."

"Thanks. Whatever you find, let me know immediately. I don't care what the time is."

"Will do." He pressed the pedal on the cart and whisked her back up to the front door of the house. "Night, Ms Greene."

"Goodnight, Samuel. Thanks for the ride."

"Couldn't have you walking all that way dressed like that. I'll get you the information as soon as I can."

She waved and let herself into the mansion. A servant hurried toward her, an apologetic expression on her face.

"So sorry, ma'am."

Ariel gave her a kind smile. "No reason to be." She leaned close and whispered conspiratorially, "I'm capable of opening my own doors."

The woman gave her a barely there one in response. A shame—everyone was so serious here. Well, most.

"Could you please send for Jackson and have him meet me in the kitchen?"

"Yes, ma'am." She bobbed then scampered off.

Ariel went to the huge kitchen and began preparing herself a sandwich. None of those puny hors d'oeuvres that had been offered would have even begun to make a dent in the hole in her stomach. "What I wouldn't give for a beer and a large steak right now."

She sighed and slapped some turkey and salami on her sandwich. Then piled on some more items—lettuce, tomato, cheese, sprouts.

"You rang, darling?"

She smiled at his tone—he was one who liked to laugh. "We need to have a pow-wow." She gestured with the knife still covered in mustard.

He stared at her plate and she slid it closer to herself.

"Wanna keep that hand, man, forget my sandwich. Make your own."

"Isn't that your job?"

She snarled silently. "My job is to keep you alive for two more weeks. I'm not your cook. Get up and fix your own damn sandwich."

He grumbled but got up, still in his tuxedo, and pulled out another hoagie.

"Ready to tell me who that man is who's been showing up everywhere we go?"

As expected, Jackson tensed before shrugging. "Maybe you have an admirer."

"Lying doesn't sit well with me. Who is he?" She cut her sandwich in half then bit into one section. *Oh yeah. So good.*

"You really want to know?" His tone was annoyed and snippy.

Taking another bite, she hooked her heels onto the rung of the stool and grunted. "Wouldn't have asked otherwise." She reached for the glass of lemonade she'd poured earlier.

"Let's make a deal then. You've been teasing me with your tight clothing and sexy walk since you arrived. You're supposed to be my girlfriend so wouldn't we be sleeping together?"

She lifted an eyebrow and swallowed her food.

"You have sex with me and I'll tell you everything."

Ariel blinked and finished off the first half of her sandwich. A bit more to drink then she wiped her mouth with the flowery paper napkin. "Fine."

Jackson seemed taken aback. "What?"

She slid off the seat and walked around the island to where he sat. "I said fine." She reached for his bow tie and undid it with ease. Swatting away his hands, she moved on to the first button of his tuxedo shirt. "I mean, you're not hard on the eyes. I could totally see myself riding your cock."

He swallowed hard and blew a breath. "Okay then. Are you sure you don't want to eat first?"

"Eat later," she purred. Capturing her lip in her teeth, she held the edges of his newly opened shirt and stared at his chest. Nice. Muscled. "Sex first." She lowered her head and inhaled the fragrance of his body then moved up until her mouth was by his ear. "Unless you'd like to stop this charade."

"What charade?" he asked, slipping his hands around her waist.

Tossing her head, she positioned herself between his legs and dragged her nails along his skin. Her other fingers teased the back of his skull. She swiped her tongue along her lips and gave him a patient smile.

"Perhaps it isn't one," she said as he jerked her closer to him. "Then again, usually when a man claims interest in me, his cock is hard." She looped her arms around his neck. "I don't give a damn which team you bat for. It matters not one whit to me. My job is to keep you alive and if that man is important to you, you need to come clean to your father. Someone will see him around too much and these people are more of a shoot first, ask questions later group."

He moved his mouth and she held up a finger by her head.

"Don't lie to either one of us. Why would you hide who you truly were?"

The kitchen door opened. She put her forehead to his and turned her head to see who it was. His mother, who smiled and backed out. Ariel put her gaze back on Jackson.

"My parents wouldn't ever understand. How did you know?"

"Don't worry about how I knew."

Jackson looked at her as if she were about to out him to the entire world. She could understand his fear — at least she wanted to — but her main goal was to get his trust.

"Is he the one?" She returned to her seat and picked up the rest of her sandwich.

Jackson pushed his plate closer to her and moved his stool so their knees almost touched when he sat once again. She chewed as she waited for an answer. It took a bit, for Jackson ate some of his own food, sitting there with his shirt open, exposing his dark skin.

"Yes. I met him in Europe and we hit it off. He was one guy who didn't seem to give a damn who my father was."

"I need his full name."

"Going to check him out?" There was more bitterness in his tone.

"I wouldn't be doing my due diligence if I didn't."

"He's a good man, Ariel."

"I hope so. I'm still running him." She spoke matter-of-factly then finished off her lemonade.

There was quiet for a bit until Jackson had eaten most of his sandwich. "So where does that leave us?"

"Did something change?" she asked.

"Besides my sexuality?"

"That didn't change."

"Are you one of those who believes they can spot any gay person?"

"Gaydar?" She laughed. "No, not even close. I am, however, observant. I don't see why things would change between us. You will need to come clean before my time here is done, though. I don't know who is coming to take my place and you need to make sure they know. It's not easy to guard someone with secrets."

He made a face. "We'll see."

She let it go. It wasn't her place to tell anyone when it was the right time to put their sexual preference out there for the public to know it.

* * * *

For the rest of her allotted time there, she and Jackson had a ton of fun, going to many different events and having a blast all the way around. She sat with him as he came out to his parents and even met Eric, his boyfriend.

However, when the time came for her to pack it up and take herself back to San Antonio, she found herself ready to be home. Standing outside her driver's door, she paused and thought about those things for a moment. Home.

When did I begin thinking of that place as my home? She exhaled sharply and climbed in. She'd just started the engine when Jackson came running out to see her. She lowered the window and waited.

"Damn, woman, you get up too early," he said with a smile.

"Shouldn't stay up so late and you'd be able to get up early as well."

His grin turned wicked and she shook her head.

"Don't want to know. Really don't."

"I'll spare you all the lewd details. This time."

She laughed. "Thank you."

"I just wanted to say thank you."

She reached through the window and placed her hand along his cheek. "You are an amazing man, Jackson. Don't ever let anyone tell you differently. Thank you."

He leaned close and kissed her, one of his own hands sliding to settle along her face. "Take care, you."

For a moment they sat there eyes closed, forehead to forehead. She opened hers first and saw Eric walking closer. "I'll miss you."

"Likewise." After one more brief kiss, he stepped back. "Drive carefully."

She waved as she put the car in gear then drove away. Before she left the drive, she stole a look back in the rear-view. Jackson and Eric stood there, watching her. She stuck her hand out again and waved one final time before getting on her way.

Ariel pulled into her parking spot at the apartment building about two in the morning. Fighting off a yawn, she got out and stretched. At the back of her

SUV, she opened the hatch and withdrew her luggage, which had tripled in size. Jackson had insisted she keep the dresses she'd needed for the outings with him, so she had those garment bags as well.

"I'm so taking the elevator," she muttered after grabbing her weapons case and making her way inside.

On the ride up, she wondered what had possessed her to take only one trip and not split it up. "Oh that's right, I'm exhausted and didn't want to go back down to finish carrying it in."

The door slid open and she stepped out, juggling the things in her arms to get the key to fit. Inside, she kicked the door shut with the heel of her boot then stumbled to her bedroom. There she let it all fall to the floor with a groan.

After another yawn, she picked up the garment bags and hung them in her closet. She stored her gun case in the safe she had then, ignoring her other bag, went to the bathroom to get ready for bed.

She'd barely gotten her hair pulled back into a braid before she fell onto her mattress and grunted as the remnants of her rapidly depleting energy left her. There was a light on in the living room but she didn't care. It was time to sleep.

When she stirred, something had changed. Alert, she tried to sort through the muddled state of her mind to discover what that was. When she shifted again, she figured it out. There was someone out in her main area.

"I'm just saying, Tuck, let her sleep." Steve's voice carried back to her, despite his attempt to keep it hushed.

"She could sleep with me beside her. She's been gone, Steve."

"Oh, grow up. Stop pouting like you're a little boy. Put that there so she sees it when she gets up."

Rolling soundlessly from the bed, she made sure she wouldn't be walking out there naked then stepped from the bedroom and leaned against the frame, arms crossed. "Good morning, guys."

Steve stood with a watering can in one hand and Tuck was messing with her mail more than anything.

"Shit. We didn't mean to wake you," Steve said. "I didn't know you were home until he came in and told me."

"It's fine. Thanks so much for taking care of everything for me."

"Not a problem, Ariel, you know that."

Tuck put down the envelopes in his hand and moved toward her. She focused totally on him. He wore a pair of his 'drop to your knees and give praise' jeans. His dark blue T-shirt clung to powerful arms and that muscled torso she enjoyed being pressed against so much. His brown gaze burned as he strode toward her and she slipped her tongue out to dampen her lips. Christ, it was nearly too much just watching him move in her direction. Beautiful. Masculine. Hers.

Whoa. Where'd that thought come from. He's not mine. We were even broken up before I left. Her brain didn't seem to agree. He was hers. Belonged to her.

Apparently her body agreed as well, for her exhaustion slipped away and her body began preparing itself for him. The feel of his thick length sliding between her legs and filling her. How it was to be under him as he drove in and out of her wetness. How possessively he held her as he made love to her gently. Or rough. Either way, it didn't matter.

Good thing this doorframe is holding me up.

He approached her, closer now, swagger fanning the heat pumping through her veins. Wanting his caress, touch, and more. Tuck paused in front of her, hooked his thumbs in his pants pockets and stared at her.

"Have fun?" His tone was cautious and she lifted an eyebrow.

"I had a blast if you must know. *He*," she said, stretching like a cat, slow and as if she had all the time in the world, "was a lot of fun.

His gaze narrowed. "Was he now?"

The man's jealous. Her grin widened. "Definitely."

"I don't believe I'm needed for this conversation," Steve interjected. "See you."

"Bye, Steve. Thanks." Ariel never took her eyes from Tuck. The sound of her door closing spurred her—or was it him—into action.

They met in a clash of lips and limbs. She purred and met his invading tongue with hers. He cupped her ass with his large hands and lifted her. She immediately wrapped her legs around him, grinding against his defined erection.

She wasn't wearing much since she'd been sleeping but those few clothes went flying and she moaned as his thick cock slid into her.

"Oh, God! Yes!"

His jeans abraded her sensitive skin and with the wall at her back, he fondled her breasts with calloused hands.

"I've missed you, Ariel." He plucked at her turgid nipples yet still wouldn't move inside her.

"So move already," she demanded, frustrated.

"Tell me you missed me."

She tried moving on him but he held her immobile with his larger body. He leaned in and took one nipple in his mouth. She whimpered.

"Tuck..."

"Tell me," he rumbled around the tip. The sensation vibrated through her and tugged at her clit, shooting more moisture to her pussy.

She gripped his hair and yanked it. "Missed you," she panted. "Now would you fucking move!"

"Patience." He tweaked her skin before soothing it with the rasp of his tongue. "Is a virtue."

"We...we both know I'm far from being anything remotely virtuous. Now, *move!*"

His chuckle was decadent. Then—thank the good Lord—he began to move.

Ariel groaned and sank into the wall as he drew back then thrust forward, beginning slow before working up in speed. She closed her eyes and held on.

He buried his face in the side of her neck as one hand dropped to fondle her clit. Fireworks exploded through her and she screamed as she orgasmed. Hard. Her internal muscles flexed and rippled around his shaft as he continued to drive into her.

Hard.

Fast.

Unrelenting.

Her breath was hard to catch but she tried. Tuck nipped her neck and roared his own release there. The heavy spurts triggered another climax within her.

"Hell," she gasped, holding him hard.

"More." He captured her mouth and carried her to the bed.

"Yes." She undulated against him.

"Welcome home," he muttered punctuating each word with a driving thrust.

* * * *

Tuck rolled over, sat up and stared at the woman who lay slumbering beside him. It was late afternoon now and they were still in her bed. Ariel rested on her stomach, arms under her pillow and the pale yellow sheet drawn up over half her ass.

As tempting as it would be to tug it down and fully expose her firm globes, he refrained. She emitted small snores as she continued to sleep. He knew she had to be exhausted. He'd been nearly insatiable.

He'd also missed her. And now that she was sleeping, he could admit that. These past few weeks without her around had been hard. She muttered and he dragged his knuckles along her cheek, smiling when she settled beneath his touch.

Tuck closed his eyes then opened them when a feathery-light touch landed upon the back of his hand. Her beautiful brown eyes waited for him.

"Hello," he whispered.

"Hey." She rolled to her side and, disappointingly, drew the sheet up to hide her breasts from him.

"Did I wake you?"

"No." She yawned. "I woke up because..." She shrugged. "Just did."

He wasn't too sure about that but let it go. "Hungry?"

"Later. Want to tell me what that was all about?"

He stretched back out beside her and propped his head upon his hand. "What? That was good—no, great sex."

"I may be exhausted, Tuck, but I'm not a fool. Don't treat me like one."

Her gaze was sharp despite her sleepiness. He stashed some hair behind her ear and smoothed his thumb along her cheekbone.

"We had broken up before I left. That, while great, was unexpected."

"I didn't agree to breaking up." He clenched his jaw until he realized what he was doing and relaxed.

"That's the thing about breaking up—you don't both have to agree. I have no time in my life for a jealous man, Tuck. I just don't."

She rolled away from him then climbed from her bed. Afternoon sun caressed her skin as she grabbed some clothing from her dresser. He watched in silence as she swiftly hid her body from his hungry gaze.

"I already work in a mostly male-dominated profession and I've busted my ass to prove myself. I did the same in the Corps. I make no excuses for what I do, nor will I ever. I go where the job sends me without complaint. If you can't accept that then this"—she gestured between them—"is right back to where it was before I left. With us over."

He sat up, frowning.

She gathered her hair into a haphazard knot on her head and stretched again.

"Over?"

"Yes. Over. I won't put up with it, Tuck."

"You want me to be okay with my girlfriend posing as another man's wife-to-be?"

"First off, that was changed. I went in as his girlfriend, not that it matters. You would have to be okay with it. Cops do it all the time going undercover. Second of all, I'm not sitting on my ass at a flower shop, Tuck. I protect people and their businesses. If Slater called me right now and said I had a job to do over in the Middle East, you can bet your fine ass I'd be suited up and ready to go before time of wheels up."

He could see her agitation growing and beckoned to her with one hand. "Come here, Ariel."

Her nose flared slightly but she moved to stand by where he sat on the bed. He swung his feet over and drew her close, inhaling the mixture of their scents on her body. Face in her belly, he shut his eyes and just held her there for a moment.

"I'm not going to apologize, Ariel, for being a possessive man. It's not in my nature. I'm easy-going but I'm not a pushover and when something bothers me, I'm not going to hide it." He pulled back and looked up at her. "Especially when it's something that concerns you."

"What's the point in bringing it up, Tuck? I get you feel the need to be possessive, that's you. Fine. But why do you feel the need to argue with me about my job? Do you have any idea how demeaning that is to me? Like you think I can't handle it, or because I don't have a dick that I'm going to be succumbing to a man's charms the instant I'm out of your sight. I don't jump everything that moves with a cock. Never have, never will. And I'd appreciate a bit of respect when it comes to my job. I'm not going out just to be some piece of eye candy and hang on a man's arm. I'm working. Twenty-four hours a day, seven days a week, I'm working. And for you to think that I'm doing this to get into someone's pants..." She began to step away from him.

Tuck tightened his hold on her before pulling her down to straddle him. He hadn't thought about it that way and part of him was embarrassed about how he'd treated her. Granted it was a small part, but at least it was something.

"I get it." He reached up to smooth his fingers along her lips. "I'm still a man who wants to protect his woman." A shake of his head. "Who *will* protect her."

"Then you don't get it," she said sadly. "I don't need your protection. I don't want to be in a man's shadow, Tuck, waiting for him to slay my beasts and keep me safe from everything. I want to be at his side, as equals."

"We are equals."

She looped her arms around his neck and rested her forehead against his. "Not if you want me one or more steps behind you, so you can keep me safe. I'm a Marine, Tuck. I don't run from, but *toward* danger. You trying to protect me and thinking you know why I'm doing something isn't going to work. I didn't grow up in a bubble and I'll be damned if I allow myself to be put in one now." She brushed a kiss along his cheek and stood up. "I'm going to get something to eat now."

He watched her walk from the room, boxers showing off her long legs and the raggedy tee hiding more than it showed but tempting him beyond reason. As he dressed in his jeans, he thought about what she'd said. And grudgingly, it made sense. Truly it did.

"Still don't mean I like it," he muttered as he padded barefoot out to the rest of her apartment in time to see her unwrapping a frozen pizza. One he and Steve had brought over for her.

He gave her a smile when she looked up at him. Her return nod was a bit reserved but he took it as a good sign she wasn't telling him to get the fuck out.

"I can't promise I'll change," he said. Tuck went to her cupboard and withdrew two glasses. "But I will try to keep what you said in mind."

"Thank you."

After they'd eaten the pizza, he led her to the bathroom and put her in the shower with him. Ariel sank to her knees in the streams of water and wrapped her full lips around his cock.

Up and down his shaft she moved, lapping the underside, swirling her tongue around the head. Torture, plain and simple, that's what it was. He wrapped his hands in her wet hair and held her where he wanted her as he thrust deep into her. Her nails dug into the backs of his thighs and she continued to watch him, with hunger and trust in her eyes.

She alternated the tightness of her suction on him and he tipped his head back to rest it along the wall of the shower. Her nails bit harder and he looked at her. She took him in fully and he shot his load—there wasn't any way to stop himself. She stayed there and took it all until he could release nothing more.

Lifting her, he reversed their positions and took her against the wall until her screams of pleasure echoed off the bathroom's surfaces. Then he took her again. And again.

Once their shower was finished and they'd dried off and dressed, Tuck sat on the couch with her burrowed against him, the television showing a baseball game. Beers sat on the coffee table and he wasn't paying much attention to anything but the woman curled up beside him.

"How are things with you?" she asked.

"Busy. I've got the investment for my architecture firm and construction company so am getting that set up to open."

She sat up and squealed. "That's wonderful, Tuck. I know you've been wanting that for a long time now." She hugged him.

"Thank you."

"Have you figured out a name?"

"Mulling a few over but I think the one I like best is Carter Architectural and Construction." He slanted his gaze to her. "What do you think?"

"Likes it muchly. Sounds very professional." She squeezed his arm as she settled back to his side.

"Thanks." It was important to him she like the name.

"Do you have logos and that already?"

He nodded, feeling a bit like a geek. "I do."

She lifted her shoulders and waved a hand. "Go get them, I want to see."

"You sure?"

"Tuck, just go."

So he did, slipping in and out of his place in moments. Then he was back on the couch with Ariel and handing her the binder. She opened it and he watched her flip through the various pages.

"So which one is it going to be?"

"What do you like?"

"I asked you first," she said.

"I know which one I like the best, I want to see if it's the one you pick." He nudged her with his shoulder. "Come on, it won't bite you." He nipped her neck. "I might, but it won't."

She burrowed closer and got comfortable, holding the book on her knees. "I like this one."

He stared at the one she'd pointed out. It was the one he'd chosen as well. "Good pick," he whispered in her ear. "That's the one I'm going with. Business cards are on their way and the building for my office should be ready this week."

"I'm so happy for you. Do you have jobs lined up or are you not to that point yet?"

"I have two that we're starting with. A house and creating some plans for another. Richard wants those done first."

"Richard? Your boss now?"

"Yes. He's supporting me on this."

"That's wonderful. I'd love to see the house when you're done."

"Count on it, babe. You can count on it."

Tuck kissed the top of her head and held her close as they relaxed with one another, just enjoying the company.

Chapter Eleven

Ariel stood at the edge of the wall and watched Connie fire the full magazine of her pistol, clear the weapon then set it down before moving the target toward them. Ariel took one of the ear protectors off her ear and released a slow whistle at the close groupings on her friend's target.

"This is why you scare me, Connie. You are one hell of a shot."

The petite woman smiled at her over the shoulder then looked back to the paper. "You can do better than this."

"But I'm not a natural. I was trained to do that. You, my dear, you are a natural at it."

Connie glanced at her again and winked. "I was trained, just not officially. But don't tell anyone. Especially Slater."

"Mum's the word on that end." She made the motion of zipping her lips and throwing away the key.

"Come on, make me a smiley face."

Ariel laughed. "A smiley face?"

"No, no. A heart. I haven't seen you do a heart lately." She hooked a clean target up then moved it back. "With the AR-15."

"Seriously? The AR?" She wiped her hands down her pant legs and cleared her throat. "Okay, I can do this."

"Dinner's on me if you do."

Ariel lifted the AR-15 from the counter space and shouldered it. Sighting down the barrel, she made a few adjustments as Connie stepped back a bit more. After putting her ear protection back on, she blew out three sharp breaths and curled her finger around the trigger. A heart. The woman wanted a heart.

Twenty shots later, it was her turn to clear the weapon and move the paper up. Sure enough, over the target's left side was a heart. It wasn't perfect but it wasn't bad either.

"You did it!" Connie said, taking the paper from her. "I love it."

"Sweetie, the things you get excited over."

"Hey, this is talent right here. Of course I'm excited over it. Plus you did it at my request so it's not like a trick or anything."

"Come on, woman. You have one more to practice on before quals."

Connie sobered. "I hate guns."

"I know. However, you know Slater's rules. Everyone has to be qualified and certified to carry."

"It seems so barbaric to me. To shoot someone. There's no finesse anymore. It's all about what you do from a distance away."

"Spoken like a woman who's good at hand-to-hand combat."

"You have to admit, Ariel, there was something amazing about the monks who defended their monasteries with nothing more than martial arts. Nowadays, someone sends a missile if they want to take something out."

"I know. Unfortunately it's the way of the world now. Guns and missiles instead of swords and martial arts." She nudged her forward. "Last one. Get some rounds in so you're used to the feel of it in your hand."

Connie picked up the revolver and loaded it. Ariel watched her as she fired it into a new paper hanging before them. The kickback was powerful but the small woman had a firm stance and it didn't rock her as much as one would have expected.

Ariel waited until she had gone through three reloads. Then she tapped her on the shoulder and pressed the button to move the sheet forward. There were a few close groupings but she was definitely better with the semi-automatic.

"Pathetic," Connie muttered, shaking her head.

"Not bad at all," she corrected. "Don't be so hard on yourself."

"Hard to stop after all these years."

She dropped a quick hug to Connie's shoulders. "I would assume so but you have to try." She didn't pretend to try to assume she understood the situation in which Connie had been raised. All she knew was that it hadn't been the easiest of lives.

"Tell me about you and that hunk. Fix things once you got back?"

Ariel tugged at her collar. "You're becoming obsessed with my sex life."

"That's because I don't have one. I have to get my kicks from listening to yours. It was hell when you were gone." Connie tossed her ear protection in the trash then picked up the weapons.

Ariel took the AR-15 and the two of them walked back to turn them in. After they'd finished that and were walking outside to her vehicle, Connie nudged her.

"So? Was he waiting with breakfast? Like, on his naked chest?"

"He rocked my world, Connie. No breakfast on his chest, though."

"Damn," she teased. "Here I was hoping for visions of chocolate sauce on those abs or honey, butterscotch, or..." She cleared her throat. "Look at that, I have visions of it."

Ariel laughed. "Come on, you sex-hungry thing. Let's grab a bite to eat. And no, not off anyone's chest."

Connie sighed heavily as she slipped into the passenger seat. "Ruin my day, won't you."

"You need to get laid, my friend."

"Tell me about it. I'm going through way too many batteries, it's insane."

She tried not to laugh, truly she did. But Ariel knew what that was like. Hell, it'd been her before she and Tuck had begun knocking boots with each other.

They went to the Hard Rock Café along the River Walk and ate an enjoyable lunch. She and Connie talked about a variety of things and after the meal was finished, they wandered along the paths working off the meal they had enjoyed.

"So, Connie. Tell me what's going on with you and Slater?"

"Me and Slater? Nothing."

"You said that really quickly and with a lot of force. Allow me to rephrase. What do you want to happen?"

She slanted her gaze to her friend whose face had turned a delightful shade of red. Connie averted her head. "Nothing. He's my boss."

"Uh-huh."

"There can't be anything more than that, even if I wanted there to be."

"Why not?" She stepped up to a vendor selling ice cream and got some for each of them. "Why can't you two have a relationship?" she asked after she had handed Connie hers.

"We work together. Come on, Ariel. I'm his bodyguard."

She cackled wickedly. "Then you should know his body exquisitely, I would think."

"Did you sleep with the man you were guarding?"

"No, but I wasn't required to do so, nor was I his type."

She paused with the spoon to her mouth. "Not his type? How are you not any man's type? Look at you, you're gorgeous."

"Well, thank you but he prefers men, so I was kind of out of luck there."

"Seriously? That hottie wants men?" She cracked her neck. "Another one taken from the women."

"Not so sure women ever had him but okay. Look, my point is, the both of you are finding each other attractive. Why not go for him?"

"And if it doesn't work out? Then what? He's my boss, Ariel. It would make things awkward."

"More so than they are now?" She pinned Connie with a raised eyebrow. "I've seen him try not to stare at you and I know your discipline is way more than ours, but I've seen the looks."

"He's a rock. He'd not bend even if I walked up and stripped before him."

"There's an idea." She nudged Connie and winked. "But I have another idea to begin with. You're going with him tonight, right?"

"I'm going. Not with him. He just wanted me there as another set of eyes. Like you. I'm not his bodyguard tonight."

Ariel frowned. "That's stupid. Who does he have in that role tonight?"

"Johnson."

There was bitterness in Connie's tone and Ariel understood it. She'd busted her hump to become his bodyguard, so to be replaced with another had to sting.

"Humph. Men. This can work to our advantage, however. Let's go shopping."

"Shopping? For what?"

"Dresses that will make his eyes fall out. You're just there as an extra set of eyes, you don't have to wear company attire. We're going to find you a dress that takes his breath away and gets the two of you together for a night of sex."

Connie's grin was evil. "I'm in."

The women returned to Ariel's SUV and headed off to one of the nicer dress stores. Ariel sat in a chair and watched as Connie and an employee went through a number of dresses until she knew they'd gotten the right one—a sleeveless, jade-green maxi dress with a scoop neckline and a tight fit that showed off all her curves. It draped and had a side slit.

"You're gonna be able to knock him over with a feather when he gets a look at you in this." She lifted a pair of jade rhinestone, stiletto, peep-toe, sling-back heels. "And these."

Connie rubbed her hands together. "Now you."

Ariel stood and went through as many dresses as Connie had before she picked hers. "I want this one."

"Good choice," Connie said.

It was silver, fitted and offered another curve-hugging look. There was a perforated faux leather detail on the side, which ended mid-thigh on her. Sleeveless and with a scoop neck, like Connie's dress, it also had the side cut out. Nearly floor length on one side, the one that boasted the leather showed a great deal of one leg. The saleswoman held up a pair of black stilettos and Ariel gave her a thumbs-up.

"Perfect."

Dresses in bags and shoes in boxes, the women left and returned to Ariel's apartment where they showered and got ready for the night. Each of them had a bracelet cuff that accompanied their dress. Hair done, they fist-bumped one another then went to the door.

Tuck and Steve were just stepping from the elevator as they left her apartment. Both men stopped and stared.

"Damn!" Tuck stepped toward them and walked around her without touching. "Where you going looking like that?"

"We're on the clock tonight," Ariel said, following him with her gaze. "Do you like it?"

"Woman, if I had my way you'd be going against the nearest wall." His voice was deep and graveled.

"And Connie?"

"Both of you are going to knock the men dead. What exactly are you doing tonight in those dresses?" Tuck touched her bare arm.

"We're just extra sets of eyes tonight."

"You two are gorgeous," Steve said.

Tuck stepped close and dropped his head to her ear. "Are you going to be in danger?"

"I'm going to a party, Tuck. I'll be back later tonight."

"I love this dress on you." He flexed his fingers. "A lot."

She appreciated him not complaining about her work. "Thank you. We have to get going."

After pressing a kiss to Tuck's cheek, she walked to the elevator and touched the button. She and Connie shared a smile as they stepped into the car when it arrived. Spinning around, she winked and blew the guys a kiss as the doors closed.

She drove them to the large mansion, which had been decked out for the occasion. Stopping before the marble steps leading into the home, she turned off the engine as a valet walked toward her. He held the door and she exited the vehicle, taking the ticket he gave her and placing it in her clutch.

"Thank you," she muttered as she walked around and found Connie waiting for her.

"Ready?"

Ariel mentally ran over the plans for the evening. "I am. Are you?"

There went that evil grin again. "Absolutely."

Side by side, the women walked up the steps and were admitted into the house. They walked down the hall to the open doors of the ballroom where the majority of the festivities were being held. They shared another look then stepped in.

As she'd intended, many males turned their heads and gazed at them. A few women as well. Ariel knew they looked good. All part of the plan. Be beautiful and keep an eye out. Without a word to one another, they set off in opposite directions, each circling their own way. As she went to the left, she smiled as she realized they had gone the way of the slit of their dresses. Hers was on the left leg and Connie's was on the right, the direction she'd ventured in.

"Thanks for coming, Ariel," Slater said as she walked up to him. His eyes widened as he took in her attire.

"Not a problem. Is there anyone in particular I'm looking for?"

Slater didn't answer and, after accepting a flute of champagne, she turned her head to find out what had his attention. Connie. Slater stared at her from across the room, eyes nearly out of his head and mouth open.

She sipped and walked up to his shoulder. "Close your mouth, Slater. Something is liable to fly in. She looks good, doesn't she?"

"What the hell is she wearing?"

"It's called a maxi dress. Make sure you compliment her on it."

"She can't work in that." His voice was rasped.

"She's here as an extra pair of eyes. We both have our comms in and that's all we're here to do. She can work just fine in it. Besides," she said with a grin. "Look at the way the men are flocking to her. No one would think she's looking for danger. And from what I hear, she's looking to get some no-strings sex."

She knew Connie would be ready to kill her but hey, she had to put it out there. Sometimes things needed a push. And pushing was something she was good at.

Slater grumbled beside her and Ariel hid her laughter. This was why she'd wanted Connie to wear something like she was doing tonight. Time for the man to see her more like a woman than just as one of his employees.

"Gonna be a lucky man who gets to take her home tonight," she said as she walked off.

"Fuck she's going home with someone else." Slater's words followed her on a dangerous thread.

Ariel didn't pause to respond, just traversed the perimeter and did her job.

* * * *

Tuck woke as the door opened. The light in the open area behind the door illuminated the woman who'd entered.

Another light flicked on and he found himself blinking up at Ariel as she pushed the door shut. "Care to explain why you're sitting here on my couch in the dark?"

"I fell asleep waiting for you to come home."

"Tuck, it's almost four in the morning."

He raked his gaze over her. Lord help him, she looked so damn good. "So it is. Did you have fun?"

She moved her hair to the side and pulled out a device from her ear then placed it on the table by the door. "It was work but it wasn't bad. There were no problems so that was a bonus."

He pushed up and went to her side. *Damn!* With her heels on, her head passed his shoulders. Trailing a hand along the smooth material of her dress, he walked around her until he was behind her. Then he nuzzled her neck and pressed kisses along the graceful curve.

"So it was a success."

"Yes."

"Glad to hear it."

She stepped away from him and moved to her bedroom, swiping the item she'd placed on the table along her way. He followed and watched her put it on the top of her dresser before removing her dress.

He swallowed hard as he stared at her in nothing but a thong and her stilettos. Her hair cascaded down her back and he longed to push it aside and kiss her skin. Lick it. Bite it. His cock stirred and he shoved his hands into his pockets.

She groaned as she took off her shoes and padded in the lacy thong to her dresser and withdrew a large shirt that covered her to the knees. "Those things were about to kill me tonight."

"Looked great in them," he offered.

She flashed him a smile. "Thanks. Look, I'm beat so am going to crash. You staying or going?"

"Staying," he said instantly.

She happily went to brush her teeth. Ariel was yawning as she came back to the bed and sat. "Hit the light then and let's sleep."

Tuck wasn't the least bit tired but he respected the fact she was and did as she had said. Besides, it was heaven being able to hold her in his arms. He scrunched closer to her as she lay spooned against him. She patted the arm he had secured around her waist and he kissed her ear.

"Night," she muttered.

Tuck didn't answer. There was no need for in the next moment, soft snores filled the air. She truly had been exhausted.

He didn't think he'd fall back asleep yet, fully intending to enjoy being with her, so he closed his eyes.

* * * *

The mouth around his cock worked up and down, teeth lightly scraping. Tuck groaned and opened his eyes. Light filtered in through the curtains yet he couldn't care at all what time it was. His attention riveted to the woman who lay between his legs.

Ariel had one hand around his balls, lightly stimulating them with tugs and touches of her nails. Her other hand was settled upon his shaft, working in tandem with her mouth, increasing and decreasing the pressure as she moved.

He sank his hands into her hair and tried to pull her up his body. "Ariel," he groaned.

"Hmm?" The vibrations rocked through him.

"Shit." He flexed his hips and drove his cock deeper into her mouth. She didn't fight him on it, just opened and took him in.

In and out he thrust and she continued to work him. His balls drew tight and he knew it was only a matter of time before he ejaculated.

"I'm about there, babe," he said.

Her brown eyes flashed up to him and she winked before closing her eyes and getting back to what she was doing. He held his position and watched her enjoy his cock. His fingers tightened in her hair as she hummed around him and he lost it. With a loud shout, he came hard, hips bucking off the mattress.

Drained, he collapsed as she moved up his body, kissing her way until she straddled his cock and stared down at him.

"That's a hell of a good morning."

Her smile was one hundred percent siren. She curved her hand around his cock and rubbed it against her wet pussy. Ariel was naked. Come to think of it, so was he. Somewhere along the way, she'd taken his pants from him. And no, he wasn't complaining.

"You know, we should be using protection," she said as she allowed the large head to slide slightly into her.

"I thought you were on the pill."

"It's not perfect. You can still get pregnant on the pill."

"Are you trying to tell me something, Ariel?" He held her hips and drew her down so he sank inside her fully.

"Oh yes." She captured her lower lip in her teeth. "Nope. Just making a statement. We should be more careful."

"That's not enough for me to stop now, babe. If you want that to happen, me stopping, so we can get some condoms for added protection, you need to tell me." He lifted then lowered her in an agonizingly slow manner.

Her eyelids fluttered. "Nope. Like I said, just making a statement."

He did it again and again until a whimper escaped her. "Good. I'll pick some up later then."

"Later. Later is good."

"Look at me, Ariel."

Her breasts heaved in time with her breathing but she opened her eyes and focused on him. "Hmm?"

He sat up and it put them face to face. Her feet were flat on the mattress and he was as far as he could be in her. Holding that position for a bit, he stared at her. Her internal muscles flexed about him, making it hard to remain still.

"I love being inside your pussy."

Her lips curled up at the sides. "I figured that."

He kissed her. "I want to fuck you bent over the kitchen counter."

She trembled even as she gasped. "You want it— carry me there and take it."

Tuck did as his lady commanded.

* * * *

"What about lambskin?"

Ariel laughed and shoved him. "Be serious."

"I am. I'm reading the box. It says for the monogamous couple seeking heightened sensitivity."

"It also says each one is individually tested to help insure reliability."

They were standing in the drugstore in the early evening.

"That's just gross. Why would I want to use one that someone else already has used?" He put the box back and picked up another. "For you."

"I don't need the added stimulation. Besides if that were the case, I have things right at my bedside for that."

His grin widened. "That's right, you do. In that case, who cares what kind we get?" He swiped a few boxes and put them in the basket. Holding up some of the stimulation oils, he looked at her with a raised eyebrow.

"You're having way too much fun," she said, shaking her head.

"I am. It's not common for me to go condom shopping."

"What did you use for your other women?"

He shrugged, not wanting to bring them into their evening.

She pushed him. "I'm only curious, it's not a trap. You are so suspicious."

"Women can be sneaky."

"I'm pretty sure you know me well enough to know I'm not like that."

"I do know that." He kissed her temple. "Come on. What else do we need. K-Y?"

She threw up her hands and walked to the end of the aisle. "You're insane."

"So, we need chocolate." He grabbed her around the waist and lifted her. Her squeal of surprise made him laugh. "Come on, woman, I need to get you some chocolate before you get crazy on me. Don't hold me up now."

"Tuck, put me down."

Instead he lifted her higher until they were nose to nose. "Kiss and I'll release you."

She ducked her head and pecked him. "Let me down."

"That wasn't a real kiss."

"You weren't specific. Put me down."

He sighed dramatically. "Fine, if you insist." He slipped her down his body, enjoying the feel of her along him.

She rolled her eyes and turned away.

He spun her back and claimed her mouth in a fierce kiss. "That's a kiss," he said once he'd left the temptation of her mouth.

Their mood stayed high as they checked out and walked back to his truck. He tossed the bag into the back of the cab and drew her close before setting his chin on her head. "What do you want to do now?"

"Take me to a park."

"A park." He opened the driver's door to allow her entrance. He climbed in as she slid over to the passenger side. "Any particular one?"

"Nope." She stretched and he was momentarily distracted by the flash of skin she exposed.

"Very well." He drove them to one less frequented than some of the others.

She smiled as she hopped out and looked around. The heat of summer had faded and they were experiencing cooler weather. He knew she was warm enough in her three-quarter-length sleeve tee and cargo pants.

Catching up to her after locking the truck, he wrapped an arm around her waist as they walked. "Something particular you wanted to do at a park?"

"Just walk. But the noise on River Walk isn't what I wanted right now." She rested her head against him as they continued along.

He understood. River Walk was impressive and amazing but because of its popularity, it was also loud.

She paused at a bench overlooking a small lake and sat. He joined her and held her tight.

"Are you going home for Thanksgiving?" she asked, rotating her foot in a circle.

Her question gave him pause. He'd not thought about that at all. "I'm not sure. Are you?"

"Nope. My family will be over in Europe."

His brow lifted. "What are they doing over there?"

"Traveling. My siblings will be flying over to meet them."

"But you can't go?"

"I used my vacation to attend Roxi's wedding. I had a lot more fun there than I would going over to Europe to be with my family." She shrugged. "Don't get me wrong, I love them, but they have a problem with me doing what I do. If I'm stuck with them, I don't have an escape route to get away when I need to. And trust me. There are times I truly need to."

He kissed and squeezed her. "I'm sorry it's rough for you."

She snorted. "Rough? Boot camp was rough on occasion. Serving in the Middle East was rough. Dealing with my family..." She sighed. "Best way to describe that is hell."

He honestly didn't know what to say after that, so he kept everything to himself.

Chapter Twelve

The look on Tuck's face was priceless and Ariel fought hard not to laugh outright at him. It wasn't easy, that was for sure. Hell, from his expression, it was like she'd imparted national secrets to him then had blown it off as if it were nothing important. After reaching out to place a hand on his arm, she squeezed it.

"It's not that big of a deal, Tuck. Don't worry. It's not like there is a giant rift between me and the rest. Some families just don't get along. We love each other and all that but it's just best I don't spend much time with them for they make me insane." She didn't like to talk about her family or what she'd come from. Wasn't a thing she found fun.

He draped his arm around her shoulders and played with the ends of her hair as they sat there, overlooking the water. She inhaled deeply then released it slowly. This was better for her. Yes, the River Walk was beautiful but the noise that came with it didn't always fit what she needed to hear.

"So, are we celebrating together then?" he asked, tugging lightly on her hair.

"We can if you're sure you're not going home. Do something for the three of us." She cleared her throat. "Unless you know Steve isn't going to be around."

He shook his head. "I can't say one way or the other. He has some things going on with..." Tuck shrugged.

Her interest was piqued. "Is he okay?"

He hemmed and hawed for a moment before the nod came. "I think so. Or will be."

"Is there anything I can help with?"

"It has to do with his wife."

She coughed. "I'm sorry, his wife?"

"I don't know the particulars, he's been fairly close-lipped on it, but yes, his wife. He wants her back and I don't know how well it's going for him."

"Damn," she said on a low whistle. "I had no idea."

"I didn't know until a short time ago. Man's like Fort Knox. Hard to get into."

She readjusted on the seat. "I say we go all out. Invite him, maybe Connie as well. They seemed to get along well, and before you say anything, no I'm not trying to set him up. But she would be a good one to have there as well so he doesn't feel like a third wheel."

"I think that would be a great idea. Your place or ours?"

"I have a table," she said with a nudge.

"Hey now. We have the coffee table."

"It's shameful. Truly it is. Two grown men who eat on the couch or standing over the sink."

"Don't forget the island." He kissed her ear. "That has stools."

"Which only get used if I'm there. Otherwise, you two are like college kids."

"We eat with you enough to insure our table manners don't dwindle."

She laughed at his comment.

"Hi, Tuck!" came a voice from behind them.

Ariel turned her head as did the man beside her. *Seriously?* Walking toward them was none other than Daisy. She'd been running—her sparkly spandex suit had some places that were a bit darker and sweat dripped down the side of her face. She had her hands on her hips as she neared. The ruby red top barely contained her breasts and the shorts, that same red, seemed unsure what their role was. It wasn't to keep her covered, that was for sure.

Tuck tensed but recovered quickly. "Daisy. What are you doing here?"

"Running, silly." She smiled. "What are you doing here? Oh, I remember you, you're the one who lives across the hall from him. Hi again."

Ariel gave her another once-over. "Hello."

It didn't go unnoticed by her that Tuck had lowered his arm from around her shoulder. Ariel prided herself on not being a jealous, insane woman like many she knew who wouldn't hesitate to make a scene, claiming she was "fighting for her man" or something like that. Ariel wasn't about to fight over a man—he either wanted to be with her or he didn't. She wasn't about to debase her own morals and make a fool out of herself. Still, that rankled and she clenched her jaw as she turned back to the front.

"What are you doing here?"

"Enjoying the park with Ariel. It was good to see you, Daisy but since you appear to be in the middle of your run, we don't want to keep you."

"Oh, it's not a problem. I was done. Just time for my cool-down stretches."

Daisy moved to where not even Ariel could avoid looking at her and began to stretch. Bending over, showing off her breasts and bouncing slow as she pretended to have a hold count. Rolling her eyes, Ariel prayed for patience. This wasn't anything she needed, nor wanted, to see.

When Daisy turned and bent over, showing off her ass, Ariel got to her feet. "I'll be by your truck whenever you can tear your gaze from her *stretches*." She strode away without waiting for him to say anything in return.

"Hey, hey. Wait a second!" Tuck grabbed her arm a few steps away from his truck and spun her toward him. "What is your deal?"

She lifted an eyebrow. "My deal? I don't have one, I just don't believe I need to sit there while she bends and stretches her ass and breasts in front of you."

He held up his hands. "I didn't ask her to do that. Hell, I didn't even know she was going to be there."

"Never said you did. You asked me what my deal was and I told you what it wasn't."

"I'm confused. Are you mad at me?"

"Tuck," she said, rolling her shoulders and pinching the bridge of her nose. "Things would have to be a lot more than this for me to be mad at you. I'm not an idiot. I know you didn't call her—hell, you could know her jogging schedule, but even if you did, I'm the one who told you to take me to a park. All I'm saying is that I didn't want to sit there and watch her almost fall out of her outfit as she tried to impress you with what you've already seen."

"So you're not mad."

The man seemed genuinely confused about that and she would have laughed had her mood not been on the fence.

"Didn't say that. I'm pissed. But I don't blame you for what happened. You're a man, so I guess it's natural for you to stare at another woman when she's dressed — and I use that term loosely — as Daisy was." She waved a hand. "I'm done discussing this. Take me home please. I need to figure out this Thanksgiving thing, plus there are some things I have to do before work tomorrow."

The myriad of emotions streaming along his face told her he still hadn't figured out if he was in the proverbial doghouse or not. "Okay." He unlocked his truck and held the door for her.

During the ride back to their apartment building, he continually turned to look at her as if completely unsure if she would turn into a head-spinning demon or not. She leaned her head back and allowed the cool autumn air to wash over her. If he didn't believe her, that was on him, not her.

Tuck walked up the steps beside her, for once not making his typical comment about how she never took the elevator. At the door to her apartment, he halted her as she put the key in the lock.

"Yes?" she asked.

"Look at me."

She did. He held the bag of their drugstore purchases in one hand but his gaze, intense, remained on her.

"I'm sorry if I upset you by looking at her."

He's cute when he's unsure. She gave a little smile. "Don't worry about it. I'm sure it's an attractive sight for many men. Hell, probably even some women." She made a face. "Not for me. I have to go, I'll see you later. Come over about eight and we'll discuss the menu for the meal. Thanks for the day, I had a blast."

She kissed him then stepped inside her place, shutting the door behind her.

Between then and when Tuck showed back up, Ariel was busy. She cleaned, showered, cooked and ate. When he walked in, she was seated at her table making a list of things to cook for the meal. It had been a while since she'd had as large a dinner as they were planning.

"Hey," she said without looking up. "Connie said she'd love to come."

"I told Steve he was coming." He stood beside her and tugged her head back. "He agreed." Tuck kissed her and she melted a bit inside.

"Good. How's he doing?"

"He was happy when I saw him last. He went to work before I came here so not sure how he is now." Tuck went to her fridge and withdrew a beer. "Want one?"

"No thanks. I have a drink." She pointed to her water.

"Water?"

"Sometimes I do drink that, you know."

He grunted.

"It's not bad. In fact, it's good for a person to drink it."

"Beer has water in it."

She shook her head and didn't bother to respond. Picking up the pencil she'd dropped when he'd kissed her, she put the tip to the paper and continued writing things she thought they should make.

"Sit down and help me here. There isn't that much time before Thanksgiving."

He plunked down the bottle and pivoted the chair to straddle it. "Show me what you've got."

Oh, the things I could say to that. Or do. You'd see what I had if I were to strip naked for starters…

* * * *

Tuck crossed his arms, watching as the backhoe and bulldozer broke the ground for his house. He was excited and had bitten off his own yell of glee. It was finally happening. This was going to be a dual purpose build. To show people what he could design and then of course build.

Most of the men he'd worked with at Richard's company had made the jump to his new one. The part that still shocked him a bit was that it had been done with Richard's complete support. He knew the man wanted him to succeed and it was a heady feeling to know your old boss had such faith and hope for you.

Richard's more than a boss, though, and I know this.

A lot had been going on since the money had been put into his account. He and Ariel didn't have as much time together anymore. That was the downside. The upside—he had his company and it was doing well right now. A few smaller jobs were coming in as well.

It was a lot different learning how to manage his time when he was the boss. The next thing on his list was to get a good secretary. One he could trust and one who had worked in the business before.

"Congratulations, Pierce."

Richard stepped up beside him. He glanced at the man and took in the impeccable three-piece suit and his cane, which was now an everyday part of his attire.

"Thank you."

"Do you have an idea how long until the house is finished?"

"A few months. We've got some other jobs to do as well, so the house is something which can be put on the backburner if necessary. I understand it will be my showpiece but I also don't want to be turning away jobs because of the house."

"Sounds like you have it all figured out."

"Getting there, sir."

"What are you doing over the holiday?"

"Having a get-together with my girl and some friends. You?" He shifted his stance and took a large breath of fresh air. This would be a beautiful place once it was all finished.

"Probably be at home, alone. The staff will make a meal that won't get much eaten from."

"Not spending it with family?"

"You know my children, Pierce. Better things to do than be with an old man who refused to let them bleed him dry."

"Why don't you come spend it with us?" The offer slipped out before he realized it.

"I wouldn't want to impose."

"Nonsense. You wouldn't be doing anything of the sort. We'll have more than enough. I insist. Come at noon, we'll be eating about one or so. Give your people the day off."

The old man smiled. Tuck ignored the happiness he saw in the eyes of his friend and mentor. "If you're sure."

"I am. We'd be honored if you'd spend the time with us."

"Thank you, Pierce."

Conversation turned to work for a while then Richard left. Tuck pulled out his cell and dialed Ariel.

"Hey, stranger," she said.

"Hey yourself, babe. How's work going?" He walked away from the noise to his truck, which he jumped in to have an easier time hearing her.

"Busy. Sounds like it is the same for you. What's up?"

"I invited someone else to Thanksgiving." He peered through one eye as if waiting for a smack to reach out and get him.

"Okay. Does this person have any allergies that I should be aware of?"

He shook his head. "Not that I know. Are you sure you're okay with this?"

"Why not? It's Thanksgiving. Who is it?"

"Richard."

"The man you used to work for, Richard?"

"That's the one. His family and him don't get along at all so he would have just been in his house barely picking on a meal his staff had made for him."

"That's not how anyone should spend this holiday. Make sure he comes. You know we planned for more food. Leftovers may be a bit less but who cares."

"Thanks, babe."

"No problem. Will I see you tonight?"

Lord, he wanted to. His cock was straining against his jeans now, just from hearing her sultry voice. Were he not worried about the men walking by, he'd pull himself out now and jack off as he talked to her.

"I hope so but I'm not sure what time I'll be done here."

"Okay."

Was it his imagination or didn't she sound too torn up over his announcement? *Keep it together, man. You're beginning to whine and worry like a woman.*

Brushing aside his brain's comment, he focused back on the conversation he was having.

"It might be late."

"I'm heading out about seven and am not sure when I'll be home. Thought maybe I'd have a chance to see you before that. Look, I know you're busy and I'm a bit behind the eight ball myself, so I have to dash. I'll catch you later."

She hung up on her end, leaving him with nothing more than a dial tone and a hard-on he could use to pound spikes with. Rubbing himself through his jeans, he made a promise to his dick. *Soon, man. Soon we'll be back inside her.*

He hopped out then went down to the work site, waving at the driver who was bringing in the mobile office. After directing him where to park, Tuck went to meet him and shook his hand after he'd jumped down. The large black man dwarfed him for size, not something that happened often.

"Thanks, Drake, for bringing this over."

"No problem. Sorry I wasn't here sooner. There's an insane amount of traffic on the roads now and I ran into a few accidents. Let me get it unhooked and I have some paper for you to sign, *bossman.*"

He chuckled and smacked him on the shoulder. "Get to it then."

Drake was quick and efficient. The men walked inside and Tuck glanced around. A few things had been dislodged during the haul-over but it wasn't bad. He took the clipboard from his friend, signed off that the delivery had been completed then returned it.

"How's things with you, man?" Tuck asked.

Drake ripped off the copy Tuck could keep and shrugged. "Not bad. Staying busy for sure. Thinking about asking Lisa to marry me."

He whistled low. "Really? You've been seeing each other for… How long now?"

"Three years. I look at it this way. We're practically married now, why not give her the ring and my name?"

"Big step."

"Not really, man. I love her. It's that simple."

Tuck grunted. "I suppose so. Just didn't think I'd ever see the day when you were that candid about your feelings."

Drake laughed. "Man, I'm not a college kid anymore, or a high-schooler where it's not cool to talk about your feelings. I'm a man, not a boy. And men keep the woman they want. I'm secure enough in myself to tell her and others how I feel. I pity anyone who can't. Life's short enough — why not spend it with the one who makes you feel like there isn't anything in this world that you can't accomplish? That's what Lisa is to me." A shrug. "And I don't mind admitting it. I should have married her a long time ago but I was still of the other mind. Now, I've changed and I want a family. With her."

Tuck filed his words away for further dissection and smiled. "Congratulations, man."

A flash of white amid the dark of his skin as Drake smiled. "Thanks. Now if I can just get her to agree to a small wedding. Like at the Justice of the Peace or something like that."

"You're totally on your own for that, man, but good luck. I hear women love that day and want to go all out."

"She's so different from all her sisters, so maybe I'll be safe."

Tuck laughed. "Good luck with that. What does she have, like, four sisters?"

"Yes, four." Drake shook his head. "Okay, let me get out of here. Call if you need more workers man — have a feeling I'm gonna be needing some extra dough."

"I'll give you a call tonight and we'll talk. I need more men."

"Excellent." He opened the door and stepped out. "Thanks, man."

Tuck waved at him. "Don't thank me, I know you're a great worker. I'll be in touch."

The door closed and he sighed as he looked around. It didn't take him long to straighten up then he sat in the back at his desk. He supposed he could call a temp agency and get a secretary while he was looking for someone permanent. Who knew, whoever made it out could turn out to be just who he needed. Pulling up the number he needed, he used his cell to make the call.

Tuck never got to see Ariel that night. After finishing up work, he called Drake and set up a time for him to stop by the following day. Then he went home and walked into his apartment at ten to nine.

"How was it?" Steve asked, muting the television.

"Exciting. How are you doing?"

"Hanging in there," he said with a shrug. "There's some leftover baked ziti in the fridge if you'd like some of that."

"I will. Thanks." He went to shower and came back out to find the place empty. Figuring Steve was in his room, Tuck dished himself up some food and heated it in the microwave.

Tired though he was, he still had a few other things to do. He made it to bed by midnight and groaned as his head hit the pillow. "Long days, short nights. It's what happens when life is good and you have your own business." He grinned in the dark and rolled over.

He hadn't been wrong, the night was extremely short. Tuck ate some toast as he waited for his coffee mug to fill. Keys in hand, he skipped the elevator and jogged down to the first floor then out to his truck. A thrill rippled through him as he saw the magnet on the door that boasted his company name.

At the work site before anyone else, he finished hooking up the electricity to a generator and taking care of the phones as well. Some of the crew began drifting in and he spoke to each of them as they came in and punched the clock.

He was back in his office at seven when the front door opened. Double-checking his watch, he figured it would be the secretary the service had said would be there by this time. "I'll be right there," he called out.

He walked out a minute later and froze in his tracks. Standing there by the door, dressed in more clothing than he'd ever seen her, was—his luck was shit— Daisy. She glanced at him with a smile on her face that faded slightly when she recognized him.

He recovered before she did and walked toward her. "You're the temp?"

She lifted her chin and nodded. "Yes. Is that going to be a problem for you?"

Probably. "Nope. Thank you for being prompt." He sent up a whispered prayer, just in case anyone up there was listening, and got to work explaining what it was he wanted from her.

Chapter Thirteen

The vibration woke her. Ariel slowly cracked her eyes open to see the red digital readout of her clock. Barely after three. She didn't want to move. Hell, she wasn't sure if she could.

"Is that your phone or mine?" Tuck's sleep-laden rumble came near her ear and she found she did have the energy to smile.

"I don't know. Where's yours?"

He flexed his hips against her. "Right here."

"Smart ass. Not what I meant." She pulled herself toward the side of the bed and fumbled for the light. "Damn," she complained, squinting when she turned it on.

Tuck had come over and they'd had a marathon run of sex, stopping only to head out to an all-night diner and eat before coming back for more. Now all she wanted was more than an hour of sleep.

She reached for a phone and stared at it. His. Not vibrating. Double crap. That meant it was hers. Stretching out her fingers, she grabbed hers and dragged it to her ear.

"Hello?"

Tuck kissed his way down her back and despite her exhaustion, her body readily responded.

"Ariel? Did I wake you?"

"Yes, Slater. You did. It's after three. Why wouldn't you have woken me?"

Tuck's fingers tightened upon her hip as he nipped her ass cheek. She squirmed.

"Better yet," she continued. "Why aren't you sleeping?"

"I needed to get some files on a project you're working on."

Tuck settled between her legs and lifted her hips a bit before placing his mouth right over her pussy.

"Oh!" she said sharply.

"Oh?" Static exploded along the lines. "What's going on?"

"Just 'Oh', Slater." She tried to concentrate—an extremely difficult task. "Why didn't you just access the mainframe and...and pull the files you needed?"

Words just weren't coming easily to her. There wasn't any way they would. Not with Tuck doing what he was to her. And with such skill. The way he feasted upon her pussy was driving her wild. He flipped himself and drew her hips down until she sat upon his face.

Shit! I can't talk coherently with his head buried between my thighs like this. Talk? I can't think.

She rocked against his thrusting tongue and bit back another moan.

"I'm not at the office."

"Okay." Her voice was breathless. "So what do you want from me?" Beneath her, Tuck's answer vibrated her clit and she fought to keep the scream inside. He held her still, never relenting in his attack.

"I need you to tell…how it…their family."

Tuck's talented tongue brought her to an explosive orgasm. She trembled and tried to find her voice.

"You're breaking up, Slater. Repeat that. Where are you?"

"…need it ASAP. Don't have…time…"

She lost the call. "Slater? Slater!" Nothing. She'd truly lost it.

Ariel's mind whirled with the possibilities of what was going on. Lifting herself from Tuck she moved his hand when he went to stop her. "Not now."

He got the tone and sat up. "What's going on?"

"I'm not sure." She dialed a number, sleeplessness falling to the wayside. "Connie? Where are you?"

"Home. It's, like, three in the morning. What do you need?"

"Slater called me needing some information. He said he wasn't at the office and he needs it quick but I lost his signal and didn't get all he said."

"Damn fool. I think I know where he went." She heard Connie getting up. "Can you meet me at the office?"

"On my way." She ended the call. "Damn."

"Ariel?"

"I don't know, Tuck. Something's up, though, and I have to go." She stood and dressed in haste. Shoving her feet into her boots, she blew some wayward hair from her face. "Go back to sleep. One of us should get some rest." She kissed him. "And, thanks."

"Want me to come with you?" he asked, grabbing her sleeve.

"No. We got this." She stepped clear from him and opened the small safe in her room, taking out her personal sidearm, her SIG. After shoving the holster in the back of her jeans, she added the pistol.

"You're taking a gun?"

"Of course I am. Gotta go. Sleep well." She blew him a kiss then dashed.

She sped all the way, praying the cops didn't pull her over. After flashing her badge at the guard, she raced up to the fifth floor of the parking garage and parked. She ran to the door, engaging the lock over her shoulder.

She'd just sat behind her desk when Connie came through the door. The woman still didn't seem rattled, although for once her eyes were slightly wide. "Anything?"

"He hasn't called back."

"Pull up the Mason–Henderson file." She sat in a chair only to pop up again. "I told him to call the cops."

Ariel frowned. "What are you talking about?" She brought up the file. "Cops? I'm lost."

"After you finished the initial assessment on them, Slater was called to do a bit more. It was when you were gone dealing with the congressman's son. Anyway, he discovered a bunch of illegal activities they were doing and got pissed. You know Slater."

Yes, she did. Slater was a man with very strong beliefs and he acted on them, sometimes without any care for consequences. Like now. Ariel opened the file and refreshed her memory of the people. They'd seemed like a nice enough couple. Looks could be deceiving and in this case, apparently, they had been.

"I do."

Connie paced. "Anyway. He found something out about them that set him off. He told me he wasn't going to do anything. That he would leave it for the authorities. Damn him, he told me!"

Now, this was a side of Connie she'd not seen before. Copying down the addresses Slater'd highlighted of a few of their buildings, she powered down her computer and stared at Connie.

"We don't know where he is yet, Connie."

Connie shot her a look that told Ariel she knew how they both disagreed with her statement. After trying Slater one more time and failing to make contact, she swore. "Let's get going."

Connie headed to the door. "I have his GPS locked." She swiped a bag Ariel hadn't previously noticed from the floor. The women made their way in silence out to Ariel's vehicle. Connie climbed in, bag at her feet, then held out the GPS and gave the address.

"Give me directions, I'm operating on short sleep here." She cranked the engine and burned rubber as she left the parking garage.

Connie tried him as Ariel drove but it never got through. Her single word directions were offset by her readying the weapons she'd pulled from the bag.

"Half a mile out," Connie said.

"Let's hoof it." It wasn't that she worried about having her vehicle potentially shot up, she didn't care about that. It was that Ariel didn't want to alert anyone they were coming and give them a chance to prepare a counterattack.

"Agreed."

The women slipped into the moonless night, fully armed, and began to move as swiftly and silently as they could. It wasn't easy going, nor was it without dangers—poisonous creatures lived out here. None of it seemed to affect Connie, however, who flowed like water over everything.

"There."

Connie's voice came through easily in the earpiece she wore. Ariel slowed and checked the direction Connie pointed. Her world was green and as she scouted the area her body thrummed with excitement, pushing the final dregs of her exhaustion away and filling her with adrenaline.

The building sat low in the desert. She couldn't see anyone on the perimeter but she knew someone was out there. It was the itch between her shoulder blades, the feeling in her gut. Something she would never doubt as long as she lived.

"I'll go right, you take left."

Ariel scouted around again. "Keep in contact. Where does it put him?"

"Hard to say. In the middle but it doesn't show floors. I called in Johnson and the twins as well."

What the heck did you get yourself into, Slater? She felt better knowing a few others were coming to back them up.

There'd been very little to go on, but she'd dug into the family as well and that was this place. The final one Slater had highlighted. So whatever she would have found, he apparently already had. The address had the brother's name on the lease and there were an awful lot of cars around for a location with zero light, not even a lamp in the lot to show people where their cars were.

"Let's go rescue our boss from whatever mess he got into."

"Yes, let's, because once he's safe, I'm going to kick his ass." Connie crouched and faced her.

She chuckled lightly at the comment and fist-bumped once with Connie before they split up. Ariel readjusted her hold on the MP-5 Connie had handed her from the bag. Her SIG was in place along her back and she also had a Mark-1 knife in a sheath on the vest she wore.

* * * *

Tuck nodded at something Drake had said as he signed the papers he held. Handing it off, he beckoned Drake with him. The site was louder today than usual.

"What's up?" Drake asked, dropping his previous thread of conversation.

"I need you to head to Broyson and pick up the trailer that was supposed to be here earlier."

"They not coming?"

"No. Apparently there was some *issue* and they can't bring it." He rolled his eyes. "We need that backhoe out of here today. Drive down, bring up the trailer and return it with the backhoe then come back." He paused. "Please."

Drake readjusted his cap, turning to spit a stream of tobacco juice. "On it, bossman."

"Thought you weren't supposed to chew."

"Don't rat me out, man!" he called, climbing into his truck.

Tuck waved as the man drove away, passing another one on the way in.

He barely glanced at Daisy who climbed out of his truck. She wore another business suit that he couldn't find fault with. She opened the back door of the cab where she withdrew two boxes of doughnuts and another box of papers.

He'd not wanted to give her his truck to use but at the moment they were spread thin, assets at three different sites. So when the need to get some things picked up had arisen, he'd handed over his keys.

Tuck had left Ariel's bed before five and hadn't talked to her since she left. He checked his phone and frowned when there were no messages from her. Pushing Ariel back from the foremost of his thoughts, he readjusted his hard hat and went to work.

His long day went past seven and he was dragging when he got home. He slumped against the wall of the elevator and dropped his head back, eyes closed.

"You changin' floors, handsome?"

The voice prompted him to open his eyes. Vanessa Creedy from…the fifth floor?

"Um."

She ran her gaze hungrily over him and stepped in. "I don't mind." Her blue gaze ran blatantly over him. "Not at all. There's room in my bed."

He straightened up realizing he'd slept past the stop on his floor and gave her a small chuckle. "What about your solider boyfriend? Don't you think he may object?"

He pressed four then the first floor button and prayed they would arrive swiftly. She was looking at him like a starving animal watching meat. Vanessa dragged her tongue along her lips seductively and trailed a finger between her hoisted breasts. "He's gone. I won't tell him."

The doors slid open and he left hastily. "Sorry, Vanessa."

"You know where to find me when you change your mind."

"Right," he muttered. "That's not going to happen."

He was unlocking the door to his apartment when a uniformed officer stepped from Ariel's. Tuck could see more inside her apartment. The man was on the phone and Tuck strode past him and stood at the apex of the chaos in her home.

He immediately found her. Ariel's face was dirty, except for the white bandages along her cheek. *What the fuck?*

"Ariel?" He repeated himself twice before she heard him and looked in his direction.

Tuck had no idea what response he expected but a head gesture wasn't it. Words, yes. That? No. He stepped farther into the room, sidestepped two officers talking and approached her. She altered her stance a bit and he saw another bandage around her upper arm.

"What's going on here?"

Three sets of eyes focused on him. Ariel's and those of the two detectives she stood with. One in a blue suit and the other in black.

"Who are you?" Blue Suit asked.

"This is my neighbor," Ariel said.

"And her boyfriend," Tuck added almost defiantly.

The detectives lifted their brows at that. Then ignored him.

"What happened next?" Black Suit tapped his notebook.

Ariel yawned. "You arrived."

Black Suit frowned. "Don't go anywhere."

"My apartment," she said. Her words were heavily laden with sarcasm.

"Ariel?" Tuck curled his hand around her neck, needing to have some contact with her. Tired eyes met his. "What's going on? This have anything to do with leaving early this morning?"

"You could say that."

"What happened to your arm?"

"Got shot." She checked her phone and he plucked it from her hand.

"Excuse me?"

She barely held his gaze. "Shot. Bullet to flesh. Shot."

He needed to calm down but it wasn't easy. She said it so casually. "And your head?"

"Tang."

He frowned. "Tang? I have a feeling you're not talking—"

She took her phone back.

"—the orange drink?"

"Nope. Knives have tangs. One caught me during a hand-to-hand confrontation."

He didn't quite understand. "What?" His mind refused to wrap around the words she spoke.

She looked at him, exasperation prevalent. "What, Tuck? I explained—"

"I'm not an idiot, Ariel. I just don't get how you're discussing being shot and having a hand-to-hand fight so casually."

"One, it comes with the job and two, I'm too damn exhausted to do anything else." She put the phone to her ear with a slight wince. "How is he? Good. Keep me posted."

He wanted to shake her. "Who's hurt?"

"Slater." She rubbed the nape of her neck and he saw numerous cuts on the back of her hand along with some starting up her arm.

Stay calm and let her explain. So much easier said than done. "Can you tell me what happened?"

She raised one eyebrow. "Haven't you watched the news?"

"No. At work all day, there's not a television out there. Then I came home."

"An underground ring dealing with the procurement and sales of exotic animals was discovered by Slater. He, being the fool he is, went in alone. He was trying to escape when he called. He didn't."

She was so matter-of-fact about it.

"So you" — he shrugged — "just went in to get him."

She held his gaze and blinked once. "Of course."

He turned away. "Of course, she says. Like I was foolish to ask." His head was beginning to throb and he rubbed his temple. "Unbelievable. I'm dating a female Rambo, that's what it is." He ran his hands through his hair and attempted to reason it out in his mind. Make some sense of the entire situation. It didn't work.

"So that's it then." When he faced her, she wasn't even looking at him. Tuck checked his watch. He still needed to eat and shower. Especially shower, to get the day's grime off.

"Would you prefer I was crying?"

Irritated with the whole thing, he nearly snapped 'yes' in response. "Of course not... It's just...a lot to take in."

A quick, disgusted snort left her. "Right, whatever. You should probably leave before I'm sitting in a way that you can't handle either."

He may have been thinking such a thing but it sucked hearing it from Ariel's lips. Not wanting to argue in front of the others, he swallowed his anger and left. After kicking the door to his place shut with the heel of his foot, he stalked to the bathroom, got in the shower and groaned in relief as hot pellets pounded into his skin.

Twenty minutes later, he stood in a pair of jeans before the microwave as he pulled out his meal. Carrying it to the couch, he put his fork into the Salisbury steak and realized how much he preferred eating with the woman across the hall.

Steve entered and the man looked rough.

"Hey."

Steve waved and gestured over his shoulder. "What's going on over there?"

"Something to do with that exotic animal ring that was shut down."

He whistled. "Wow. I saw part of that on TV. They were hauling one man out of there on a stretcher. Lots of bodies in bags, too. She okay?"

He hadn't needed to hear that. "She had some cuts." *And a fuckin' bullet wound.*

"Good."

Steve walked on and Tuck ate a bit only to put the fork down. Tasted like sawdust. Or cardboard. Perhaps both.

Everything in him wanted to head back over there. Hold her.

He got up and made his way to the door and opened it. Beer dangling from one hand, he stared into her place as it sat wide open. Men he didn't know, dressed similarly to Ariel, all in black, stood near her. One bent close as the duo whispered.

Tuck was entering her apartment before he realized it and had approached the foursome. All of them looked at him.

"Need something?" Ariel asked.

"Yeah." He gripped her chin and kissed her. Claimed her before all the men—and women—occupying her place. Her brown eyes sparked at him and he—without looking away from her—said, "Could you give us a minute?"

Each man gave her a fist bump before leaving them in relative privacy.

"Have a need to make a statement," she said drolly.

"Yes." He stepped so her legs were between his. "I don't like so many men around you."

Her eyes narrowed briefly and he waited for some remark but none was forthcoming. She yawned and he — carefully — cupped the back of her head, pressing her to him.

"Have you eaten?"

"Yesterday with you." She turned her head, hair gliding along his skin. "Oh, wait. That's not true. I split a power bar thingy with Connie."

He furrowed his brow. "Where is Connie?"

"Hospital with Slater waiting for him to wake so she can kick his ass."

He had so many questions. "How long are they here for?"

She shrugged. "No clue."

"Who's in charge?"

Another yawn. "Blue suit. Bald head. Name's Jack."

Tuck located him and whispered, "Be right back."

He waited for the blue-suited, bald man to finish with the officer he spoke with.

"Yes?"

"How much longer is this going to take?"

"Who are you?"

"Her boyfriend."

He lifted his bushy eyebrows. "We're in the middle of an investigation."

"So conduct it at your station. She's wiped."

"We'll be in touch." Jack whistled. "Let's go." He stared at Tuck. "She thinks of anything else, have her contact me."

"Sure thing." He helped shoo them out and locked the door behind the last departing person. "Shower and I'll fix you something to eat."

She slid off the table and rotated her booted feet. Tuck realized how exhausted she was. He knelt down and unlaced her black boots before removing them.

"Can you handle the rest?"

"Uh-huh." She stumbled to her room and moments later the shower came on.

He made her a cup of soup. Quick and easy. Not to mention, it wasn't anything heavy. Ten minutes later, he pushed into her bathroom.

"Ariel?"

"Hmm?"

"You awake?"

"Uh-uh."

He moved the curtain and the sight of her wet, naked body had him repeating *hands off* through his mind. She leaned in the corner, her eyes closed. Tuck shut off the shower, wrapped a towel around her then assisted her to the kitchen table.

As she sat, he nuked her soup then placed it before her.

"Drink up."

She didn't move.

"Drink up, Marine."

She reached for the cream of chicken and drank it down as he stared at her bandaged arm and face.

"Come on," he encouraged as she lowered her head to the table.

Eyes barely open, she didn't protest when he guided her back to her room and put her to bed. She was asleep almost instantly and he sat beside her, just watching her for a while, thinking about how he was going to talk through this because he wasn't sure he could do it without yelling. He wasn't sure—correction, he was positive—he didn't like her in danger.

Chapter Fourteen

Ariel smiled at Connie as they worked together to get the Thanksgiving meal ready. A few people had shown up and they were expecting more to dribble in throughout the morning. They'd set the meal time for one, but most they knew would be there early.

There was a bit of strain between her and Tuck. There was something she'd not told him that still bothered her, aside from the fact he was still upset over what had happened when she and the others had gone after Slater. He'd told her she wasn't a Marine any longer, she didn't need to go acting like one. She shook her head—he just didn't understand. He wanted her to stay behind the desk and do her work that way and it was hard for him to reconcile she did more than he'd first assumed. Regardless, she was looking forward to spending this holiday with him.

Slater was there—Connie told the man he was coming so she could keep an eye on him. Steve was chatting with Slater. Tuck would be arriving later, as would his old boss and mentor.

This morning she and Connie, who'd stayed the night, had moved her living room around to make more seating room. The table had been extended and was set for the meal, the fire-engine red candles in the middle waiting to be lit.

The entire place smelled like heaven and she was having a hard time not swiping more food.

"Good thing you got so many olives," Connie said.

"I know, I think we've eaten an entire container ourselves so far."

Connie laughed and poured the chocolate filling into the pie shell. "At least one. Maybe one of black and one green."

"Could be. All I know is they're tasty and I have no shame."

"Makes two of us." She licked the spatula. "Apparently that extends to chocolate as well."

Ariel chuckled and went back to chopping the rest of the veggies to refill the plate people were snacking from. "Ain't nothing wrong with that, Connie. What with chocolate being one of the food groups." She popped in a piece of celery. "At least in my world."

"I like your world, sounds good to me." The dish went to the sink and Connie got to work on something else.

"Knock knock!" a man called out.

Ariel looked up and saw an older gentleman in the doorway. She'd left her door open. She wiped her hands and went to meet him. "You must be Richard, it's a pleasure to meet you. I'm Ariel."

He took her hand and bent over it. "Thank you so much for inviting an old man you don't know to dinner."

"The more the merrier. Come on in. Tuck should be here later." She took the bottle of wine he offered and led him in. "Everyone, this is Richard." She passed the gift to Connie who placed it on the counter as introductions were made.

The nearer it got to one, the richer the scents were in the apartment. They were sitting around, drinking wine and laughing when Tuck showed up. Connie nudged her in the side and said, "Who the fuck is that with him?"

Ariel had to pull her gaze from Tuck who stood in the doorway looking too damn good for her own sanity in order to answer Connie's question. *Are you fucking kidding me?* Standing just slightly behind him was none other than Daisy.

She flashed to his face and he had this expression like he was asking her not to make a scene. Ariel seethed but something else clicked for her and she returned Connie's hand squeeze before she spoke. "Hi, Tuck. Glad you made it. We're about to eat."

He stepped in the apartment and looked around. "There was something I had to take care of at work. And I ran into Daisy who said she didn't have anywhere to go for the day. I told her the more the merrier."

Knew those damn words would come back to haunt me. I can't believe he brought one of his women to my place for Thanksgiving. Guess it explains something else, though.

Pasting a smile on her face, Ariel toasted them with her glass. "Make yourselves comfortable."

"Are you okay?" Connie whispered.

"Peachy."

"You know that was your response after you got shot and I asked you how you were."

She lifted her shoulders languidly. "Feel like I just took another bullet, in a way."

Talk resumed after Tuck made introductions. He got Daisy some wine and carried his own glass to a chair near Ariel. So much wanted to stream from her mouth but she locked it behind her teeth. It was a day for giving thanks. She wasn't going to ruin it or make it uncomfortable for the others merely because she was pissed. And boy was she pissed.

Tuck got her alone in her room while people were eating—she stepped out from her bathroom to find him there. The door behind him was closed. She took a moment and made sure her skirt was still fine. Sure, she knew it was, but it gave her something to do for a minute.

"Thank you," he said.

She watched him. "For?"

"Not making a scene when Daisy showed up."

Her head buzzed and she ignored it. "She didn't *show* up, *you* brought her."

"She said she didn't have anywhere to go today."

Her eye twitched. "So you thought you'd just bring her along with you. How sweet."

"It's Thanksgiving."

"Didn't see you bringing any homeless folks back with you. They don't have people to be with either." She glanced around. "Where are they?"

Tuck reached for her and she glared at him. "Don't be like this."

"Like what? Pissed you bring a woman who's shared your bed to my apartment? Pissed you didn't tell me she was working for you, driving your vehicles, what?" She blew out a breath. "You know what? I don't care. I have guests out there and I'm not about to get into this with you. Not now."

She walked out on his shocked expression and rejoined the group eating. Connie shot her a look and she gave her a nod, letting her know she was fine. Her friend didn't appear all that convinced.

Ariel picked up a conversation with Steve and did her best to ignore the issue before her with Tuck. She'd made sure to sit away from him and kept people between them. To be near him and his woman wasn't at all something she wished to do. Thankfully everyone ignored the slight tension between her and Tuck, continuing to keep the mood light.

It was late when people began to file out. Slater went to the door. "Wait, Slater," Connie said.

Their boss turned and frowned but didn't leave. Connie looked at her. "You sure you don't need my help in cleaning all this up?"

"No, go. Take care of him, I got this."

"I'm sorry she showed up."

"He's the one who brought her," she said, anger flashing anew.

"I'll see you soon."

"Take care."

Connie gave her a smile then went to the door where she and Slater exchanged words on their way out. Ariel rubbed her temples. Even now, on Thanksgiving, she knew Connie wouldn't let down her guard. She was still livid over Slater having gone in by himself and she'd not been shy about letting him know.

Tuck waited until they were alone then shut the door to her place and approached her. She watched him move across her room in the reflection of the window she stood before as she got ready to load the dishwasher.

"Can we talk now?"

That's not the question you should be asking, Tuck. You should be wondering if I can talk without losing my shit and kicking your ass. She skimmed her teeth with her tongue and shrugged. "So talk. I'm busy."

"What are you pissed about?"

The dish clattered to the countertop. "Really? That's what you're starting with?" She gripped the edges and took several deep breaths.

"Yeah. You haven't been happy since I brought her here."

"How rude of me," she sneered. "To not be doing cartwheels when a man I'm dating brings a woman he's fucked in the past to my place for Thanksgiving dinner." She whirled around. "Did you plan on telling me she worked with you and you'd given her carte blanche to drive your truck around San Antonio? Or was that something you hoped I'd never find out? At least this explains what you had to do at work this morning."

"How did you find out she was working with me?"

"Answering all that with a question. Wow. I saw her getting out of your truck. And I've seen her getting out of a company vehicle. Typically, she drives your truck, though. Plan on answering my questions?"

"She was sent by the temp agency." He shrugged. "She's good."

"I bet she is." Her words were icy.

"Is that what you think? I'm fucking her?" He glowered.

"I think you didn't think enough of our relationship to tell me you had hired a woman you'd fucked right before we got into bed together. And…nope. I'm not doing this again. I won't. I won't. I *won't.*" She wiped her hands off and walked across the floor, heels clicking, then opened the door. "There's nothing else to talk about. We're done."

"You're breaking up with me? Over that?"

She crossed her arms and glared back at him. "You came bursting in here the other day pissed because I did my job and there were men around me."

"I still am pissed. You were shot and acted like it was nothing. Then yes, you had your men around you. Yes, I was pissed. And as stated, I still am."

"So it's okay for you to be pissed I was doing my job but I can't be pissed you're working with a woman who's spent time nude in your bed, who we've also run into at a park where her blatant advances would have been visible to a blind man, and now I know she's allowed to drive your truck and who knows do what else with" — she gestured at him — "all that. Good luck with that."

"I didn't think it was —"

"I get it. You didn't think it was anything I needed to know. Which is not a good thing."

"So what, you're supposed to tell me who I can and can't hire?"

"So you've hired her now? I thought the temp agency sent her over."

He swallowed. "That's how it started."

Ariel prayed for patience. "Great. No, I'm not saying I can say who you hire for your business. I have nothing to do with it, but out of respect you could have mentioned that to me. It's obvious there is none."

"I can't believe you're making such a big deal out of this."

Her smile was feral. "Chalk it up to me being a woman and hormonal. Now get the fuck out."

He frowned but she merely lifted one eyebrow and pointed. With a curse, he shook his head and went by her. Ariel took immense pleasure in kicking the door shut behind him.

* * * *

"She has a point, you know."

Tuck glared at Steve, not wanting to hear whatever he was saying.

"So you've said," he growled. "Why are you on her side?"

"I'm not. Just pointing out she had a point."

"It's my business. I can hire whomever I want. And, even better, I can do it without getting her permission."

"No argument."

"I don't need her permission!" he reiterated.

"Sure don't."

He crushed his beer can in one fist. "But...she's acted like I had to. Or should have."

Steve ate his final taco. "Really? When?"

Tuck scowled at his friend and roommate. "What do you mean when?"

"From what you've said went down, she said that wasn't it."

"Support?" He lifted a brow and stared at the man.

"I'm your friend, Tuck, but I won't side with you over something *you* told me yourself she *didn't* say." He wiped his mouth. "I'm her friend as well."

Words he knew were true but right now didn't want to hear. He scratched his arm. "Have you seen her?" God, he sounded pathetic.

"A few times right after Thanksgiving. Nothing for a while now."

He hated his friend. Was that lame? Probably, and no, he didn't give a damn. They were three days from Christmas. He'd not seen her at all since she'd kicked him out and he could no longer get in her apartment.

Whatever it was she'd put him on—in her system—she'd since removed him.

Tuck bit back his question, although from the smirk on Steve's face, he'd anticipated it already.

"Yes, I could still get in the last time I went there." Something flashed across Steve's face and he wanted to ask him what it was about.

He muttered very unkind words.

"Did you think she was going to continue allowing you unlimited access to her place?" His silence was damning. "You also think she didn't mean it about the break-up."

"Fuck you, Steve."

"Not my type, man." He threw away his plate. "I hope you figure it out before you lose her forever."

Forever. That was a word he didn't want to think about in terms of not having Ariel in his life. "I ain't chasing her. There are plenty more fish in the sea." His remark was stubborn and defiant.

Steve snorted and raised his eyebrow. "Right. Don't think you'll find any more like her. Think about that. Kind of hard to get the woman you're building a house for to live in it if you're not with her anymore." He left.

More curses streamed from his mouth. Steve was one hundred percent right. About her and the house. *Thump!* He started and stared at the door from which the noise had come through.

What the frack? He went to the door. Opening it, he frowned at what he saw. Movers. Four men and the noise had been them setting down her couch—one must have dropped his end. There was no mistaking it was hers, he'd fucked her enough on it.

"What's going on here?" he demanded.

"Moving." The men laughed.

Tuck was far from amused. He went to her door. "Ariel?"

"Ms Greene's not here, man."

Facing the one who had spoken, he said, "Where is she?"

"Not a clue. We were hired to move her. Excuse me." He went by Tuck and shut the door behind him.

Tuck couldn't believe it. Back at his apartment, he grabbed his cell and called her. Nothing. Went to her voicemail.

"Ariel, it's me, Tuck. Call me. I see you're moving." He ended the call.

The next time he left, her place was empty and the guys were leaving, being replaced by a two-woman cleaning crew who entered as the movers vacated. The door clicked behind them, sounding so final.

He rubbed his chest, unpleased with the empty feeling seated there. *Okay, so I thought she was having a tantrum. Pissed over Daisy.* He rolled his eyes. *What kind of guy pines over a woman who has made it clear she doesn't want him?* Him for one. Tuck thought about how Steve was fighting to save his marriage and keep the woman he loved. And Drake—he wanted to let the world know he was Lisa's man. They were okay with admitting how they felt.

He palmed his keys then went to his truck. Behind the wheel, he frowned at the lingering scent of Daisy's perfume. Doing his best to ignore it, he drove all the way out to the site of his new house and walked through the three thousand plus feet of space. A lot of time and vision had gone into the drawing of these plans. And every second of it had been after he'd met Ariel.

Despite the chill, he sat on his tailgate and overlooked the property. This would be his. A truck rumbled up the dirt drive and parked next to him. Drake got out and zipped up his coat before joining him on the tailgate.

"It's three days before Christmas, man. What are you doing out here? Shouldn't you be at some swanky holiday party? Kissing your woman." A grin. "Or *women* under the mistletoe?"

Tuck stared at the tips of his boots. "Have no parties to go to. Got no woman. She dumped me on Thanksgiving."

"Shit, that's cold. You still pining after her? Gonna get her back?"

"Nope. She moved. Not a fucking clue where." He stared at his home and accepted he had seen Ariel as the one sharing it with him, as he'd drawn it on paper. Imagined her subtle touches once it was finished to take it that final step from house to home.

Now what do I have? A house, no woman and only memories.

"Damn. You really fucked up."

"Thanks," he replied sarcastically.

"Sorry, man. Just calling it like I see it."

"Great." He gestured with his hand around the area. "What brings you out here? As you pointed out, it's three days before Christmas."

"Left some of Lisa's containers out here and she needs them for leftovers. So here I am."

"I saw them in there. Four I believe. In the front room."

"Yes." He made a fist pump. "Thank God they're still there. I didn't relish having to explain to her that I lost them. The woman can be downright vicious."

Tuck laughed. He'd met Lisa—and enjoyed spending time with her very much—but it was highly entertaining for him to think of big Drake scared of her. She was barely a buck-five soaking wet. His little firecracker, Drake called her. Words usually accompanied by a wink and lustful grin.

"I'm sure you can find a way to appease her."

Drake smirked. "Man, she's appeased *every* night."

Tuck smacked his leg. "Shit, you're right. I gotta get going. If you're here that means I need to swing by and make her smile. We always do the appeasing when you're not there, but it's good of you to acknowledge that she's getting it every night."

With a punch to his shoulder, Drake said, "You wish, man, you wish. All righty, I'm outta here, getting dishes and getting home." Drake hopped off only to turn back. "You got plans for dinner or do you want to come over? Lisa would love to see you."

He slapped him on the shoulder. "Thanks but there's somewhere I have to be."

"I'm out!"

"Bye, Drake."

"Hey, bossman."

He stared at his friend and employee who peered at him over the cab of his truck. "Yeah?"

"Merry Christmas."

This time the smile came easier. "Same to you, man. Same to you. Give Lisa a kiss for me."

Drake waved, then drove closer to the house, leaving his truck running while he jumped out and got what he came for then left, honking on his way out. Tuck hung out for a short time before sliding off and heading out.

As he realized how comfortable Drake was in his relationship with Lisa and could handle teasing like that, he was in the Starbucks drive-through. Tuck knew he wasn't that good for he'd been pissed just by Ariel having men around her he didn't know. He needed to change. Once he'd been served, he headed for his next destination.

Sipping his coffee, he stepped into the elevator car then pressed the button for his desired floor. In the corner he waited as the music—holiday, of course—played. He walked to the door after departing the car, pausing at the logo that he was used to seeing pinned to the lapel of Ariel's suit coat or shirt before pushing through. Connie sat behind the desk and she blinked before watching him with no sign of recognition.

"Welcome to Prometheus Protections. May I help you?"

"Is Ariel here, Connie?" He approached her desk and placed his cup on it.

She barely blinked. "Ms Greene is not available."

"I'll wait."

"We close in fifteen minutes."

"Great." He went to the leather couch and sat, ensuring he kept an eye on the door.

"Sir, I'm going to have to ask you to leave now. We're closing for the night."

He peered up from the magazine that had snapped up his attention. Rotating his empty coffee cup, he stared up at her. "Where's Ariel?" He wasn't leaving until he got some answers.

The door behind Connie opened and Slater stepped through. "Let's go, Connie. I'm done for the night. Oh... What are you doing here?"

"Looking for Ariel." He replaced the magazine.

Slater approached them. "Didn't she tell you Ariel's not here? Connie?"

"I told him she was not available. The standard answer when one asks about someone who isn't here." There was no remorse in her tone.

Tuck stood. "Could have told me she wasn't in the building."

"You didn't ask." Her voice was bland. "I will be by the door."

Slater whistled low. "That there, my man, is one woman you don't want to be pissed at you. And it seems you've managed to do that."

"Why would she be mad at me?"

"She's upset because you insulted Ariel by bringing that woman to Thanksgiving."

Tuck exhaled and tossed the cup into the trash. "Where is she?"

"Ariel?"

He flexed his fists. "Slater, I'm not in the mood."

Before he could blink, Connie had inserted herself between them. Had he not heard from Ariel about how she was, he would have considered laughing at her belief that she could stop him had he any wish to harm Slater. He sidestepped a bit but she moved fluidly with him.

"Tell me where she is." He remained focused on Slater.

"Can't."

His growl rumbled up from his chest and he'd taken one step before pulling up.

Connie had drawn a firearm and it was aimed at his head. *Shit!* He dropped back, turning desperate eyes to Slater.

"Connie, I think I'm—"

"Back away, sir. It is my job to assess threats and protect you. That's what you hired me for."

"I'm not a threat." Tuck stepped back a few more. "I just want to know where she is."

"Connie, put your pistol away," Slater said.

"He needs to leave."

Tuck was of the same mind. Hell, he'd shared beer, wine and laughs with this woman and none of it mattered. Her job did. Similar to how Ariel was—the job came first, always. He headed for the door and asked again. "Can you tell me?"

"She was called up. Activated, so we haven't any clue."

Slater's voice trailed him to the door. He opened the door and passed through before facing the duo. Connie still aimed her sidearm at him.

Damn woman is all about business.

"Thank you." He left and, in the elevator, expelled his breath as he realized he'd been extremely close to getting shot.

That was a new one for me.

By his truck, he leaned against the hood and linked his fingers. "I'm not giving you up without a fight, Ariel Greene. I will find you."

And he had plans to keep her in his life this time. As Drake had said, it was time for him to be a man and go after the final thing to make his life complete.

Ariel Greene.

And he knew it wouldn't be easy. He would have to compromise with her but to have her, beside him...forever? He was ready to walk through hell if that's what she required of him.

Tuck got in his truck and started the engine to go to the apartment. As he stopped at an intersection and waited for the red to change, he felt a seed of hope begin to grow within him. It finally switched to green and he accelerated. Bright lights had him narrowing his eyes against the glare as they approached him.

Crunch!

Chapter Fifteen

Ariel stepped from the shower and paused at the sight of her second lieutenant standing there. Despite only wearing a towel, she straightened to attention. They'd just gotten back from patrol and she'd been filthy. Not to mention looking forward to—and desperately needing—the final shower she'd have before landing stateside.

"Ma'am?"

"The colonel wants to see you."

"I'll report as soon as I dress."

"See that you do." She turned and walked to the door. "Great job, today, Sergeant."

"Thank you, Lieutenant."

She was left alone. Ariel wiped a hand over the fogged mirror and stared at her reflection. She'd been activated to take the place of this unit's person who'd been KIA. Today, she'd been on point for the patrol.

I hated this damn country when I was here before. My opinion on it hasn't changed.

She donned her clothing and laced up her boots before fixing the fall of her pants. Once her wet hair had been drawn back into a tight bun, she left the shower and headed to her commanding officer's tent.

"Sergeant Greene reporting as ordered," she said once she'd stepped inside.

Colonel Leaf waved her forward while he spoke to his aide. She stood at attention, waiting.

"At ease, Sergeant. I'll be right with you."

Smoothly, she readjusted to parade rest. People had begun to pack up the colonel's items. They were rotating out tomorrow — she'd only been here for eight weeks. Again, not that she minded. At least she got to go home when they did instead of having to stay.

"Have a seat, Sergeant."

She did and stared at Colonel Leaf. He was a proud man — he dyed his hair black as he desperately tried to hide the gray. His current dye job wasn't the best for she could see some places he'd missed. They'd had a rocky start but she believed they'd come to an understanding of sorts.

"A message for you. I thought best you read it after the patrol." He slid a folded sheet to her.

Uncertain, she took it, sat back and read.

Please advise Sgt Ariel Greene that Tuck Carter has been severely injured in a car accident. Prognosis uncertain. Slater

Her stomach revolted and it was only with great control that she avoided puking her guts out. She trembled as the words tumbled around in her head. The need to be at Tuck's side slammed her with incredible force. *Shit.* Ariel folded the sheet again and crushed it in her palm.

Colonel Leaf studied her before resting folded hands on the desk. "Are you okay?"

"Yes, sir."

"Very well. You are dismissed."

Ariel was in a bit of a daze as she walked back through the camp to find and utilize her rack. Tuck. Sitting on the narrow bed, she dropped her head in her hands. She missed him and wanted to see him for herself. *Prognosis uncertain.* Those weren't good words. What had happened? So many questions were there and she had no way of getting answers now. She was leaving tomorrow and would be home shortly after that.

Home? More like another place to lay her head. All of her things were in storage. She made a mental note to call Connie or Slater to find out what hospital Tuck was being held at. Flopping back, she closed her eyes and called up a mental recollection of the man she'd desired since the first time she met him.

Big. Muscular. Still, so gentle with her. *Sometimes. He wasn't gentle in the museum when he took you so many times,* her subconscious reminded her. It was true but she'd taken what he'd given her with pleasure. Much pleasure.

It was hard to imagine her big, strong man in a hospital bed.

Yours? Her brain chimed in. *He's not yours any longer. You broke up with him.*

True. She had. *Doesn't mean I don't still care.*

And she did care. Breaking it off hadn't been an easy decision for her to come to, especially not given the depth of her emotions toward him. However, respect was necessary and his neglecting to mention that whore to her had been bad enough. Didn't help that she'd seen Daisy using his truck. Hell, he'd said to her he didn't like anyone driving his vehicle, and this woman had—it appeared—carte blanche to do just that. Ariel had seen her on more than a few occasions behind the wheel.

That alone would have been difficult enough but she'd dealt with it—the uncertainty, insecurity and all the other negative feelings that came with it—all the while waiting for him to tell her he'd gone and hired the woman to his company. He never had. It was disappointing that he wouldn't let her know. More than that, however, it hurt. Why didn't he want her to know? Was there something between him and Daisy?

The proverbial straw that broke the camel's back had happened when he'd brought her for Thanksgiving. It had been too much and she hadn't been able to just look the other way anymore.

She readjusted and tried to find a comfortable spot. Her body, while being physically tired, didn't slow down the wheel in her mind about Tuck's injury.

"Greene! Volleyball. Five min."

She waved a hand in acknowledgment. *Well, I was clean for about fifteen tics.* She gave herself another three before pushing up from the bed. She stripped her blouse and headed out in her tank top. She couldn't be shirtless like the men but she would do what she could to stay cool. Bottle of water in hand, she slipped on her sunglasses and made her way to the edge of their makeshift court.

"Where am I?" she asked.

Side and position realized, she did her best not to think about Tuck. There wasn't anything she could do from where she was anyway. The feat wasn't one easily accomplished, but she managed.

* * * *

"Yes, ma'am. I made it back just fine." Ariel stood at the conveyor system in baggage claim, waiting for luggage, and spoke to her mother.

"That's wonderful to hear, dear. I do worry so when you are off playing solider." The comment was flippant.

Ariel tapped her forehead and paced, trying to keep her retort inside. This was why she didn't spend much time with her family. It always went like this.

Mrs Julianna Greene was stubborn and set in her ways. One of which was her belief that men went to war to fight. Not women. And especially not *her* daughter. Women were to stay home and raise a family.

She knew this happened even more because she was born into money and didn't need to do such things. Hell, according to her mother she shouldn't even be working period, but planning parties and giving orders to the help.

"Now," her mother said. "When will you be home?"

Ariel could picture her. She would be standing in her room, possibly on the balcony, staring out over her domain and clapping her hands as she envisioned all the people she would control. "I'm not coming home. I have a job to get to."

"There's this doctor I want to introduce you to. Now, he's merely a surgeon, not a specialist. However, he's mentioned thinking about becoming one in the future. Very easy on the eyes. I've shown him your picture and he's anxious to meet you."

She needed a drink. A big, stiff one. "Again, although I'm sure you talking over me was perfectly deliberate, let me reiterate this. I'm not coming home."

"Don't you sass me. You're not gone playing in the sand, you're home and therefore you will come home."

I love her. Truly, I do. Right? "I have a job."

"Why do you have to fight everything, Ariel? Can't you just once not make things difficult for me? It's your father's seventieth birthday three days from now and I *expect* you home to attend the bash we're putting on. I know you wouldn't disappoint him." The words implied she'd hurt her mother. *Shit, shit, shit!* She'd totally forgotten that. There was no way she could skip it, not being in the country as she was. Looked like she had to book another flight. Of course there was still time to get a hotel and at least drop in and see Tuck.

"I'll be there the day before."

"Can't you just come today? I have the seamstress on call in case you have nothing to wear but less than twenty-four hours isn't much time for you to get a proper wardrobe."

Translation—no matter what she wore, it wouldn't be good enough for Mrs Julianna Greene.

"My closet is full of clothing." The light blinked and the warning sounded. *Finally.*

A heavy sigh. "All outdated fashions."

"Mother, do not think you can toss me into some fancy clothes and marry me off. The clothing will be fine for Daddy's party."

"Were you not listening to me? I want you to meet this doctor. He will be at the party."

"I'm coming for Daddy's party. Not for a date."

The first of the bags began appearing.

"No harm in doing both. You're not getting any younger, you know. You need to get married and have a child before you're too old. Now, when you're here make sure we dispense with talking about you playing in the dirt. He wouldn't be impressed by that."

"You mean my being a Marine?"

The sigh said it all. "I expect you to act like a lady who's had a good upbringing."

She rolled her eyes and reached for her desert camouflage bag. "So, however I normally act…"

"The opposite. He's a good man for you and would make a great father. He wants three kids. Two boys and a girl. No pets. He knows you enjoy cooking and that's something he approves of."

Of course he does. She prayed for patience. "I have to go, Mother. I will see you in two days."

She hung up and groaned. That short call had been more exhausting than her past eight weeks. After shouldering her bag, she walked out to a waiting taxi. She had already reported in and had been dropped back to active reserve status.

The taxi dropped her off at a hotel and she tossed her bag onto the bed once in her room. Then she called Slater to find out what had happened and where Tuck was.

Her mood was somber as she stepped out of the Charleston International Airport and walked to where her rental would be waiting for her. Tuck was comatose and the respirator attached to him made him seem so fragile, she'd spent most of her two days before coming here with him.

After unlocking the door to her Chrysler 300, she put her bag in the trunk then got behind the wheel. She didn't want to be here. She wanted to be with Tuck.

"Not entirely true, I want to see Daddy." She pulled away from the lot and began the trek to the house she grew up in. "It's everyone else I don't want to deal with."

She spent her time on the road convincing herself she wouldn't allow them to draw her into any kind of argument. She would be pleasant. After all, it was only a day and a half. She could handle that.

Outside the gate of her childhood home, she paused before turning up the long paved drive. At the top she saw the large house with the six pillars. Rolling her eyes at the overstated opulence, she took her foot off the brake and began heading up.

She parked in front of the six-car garage and got her bag before striding to the door. It swung open and she smiled affectionately at the man standing there.

"Porter!"

"Ms Greene," he said with a smile. "Welcome home."

She hugged the reed-thin man and pressed a kiss to his weathered cheek. "How are you?"

"Fine, thank you."

Porter was the one person from her childhood she recalled with any fondness. He allowed her to tail him and regaled her with tails of his life in the Marines. She'd joined because of him.

"Where is everyone?"

"Atrium." He winked. "Shall I alert her to your arrival?"

"No, no." She held up her hands and waved them vehemently. "Definitely not necessary to do that."

His nod was one of understanding. "It's always a blessing to see you." He walked her to the stairs and parted ways there.

She watched him walk away. A bit older and a bit slower, but she'd bet anything he was just as sharp. Jogging up to the next floor, she went to then pushed open the door of her room and stepped inside. Instantly her eyes hurt—pink and lace. What every good young girl desired. Especially a debutante. Or so she'd been informed by her mother. Eventually she'd learned to tune out the color and ignore how offensive it was to her.

After debating changing for a while, she finally decided to stay how she was dressed. *So much for avoiding confrontation*, she told herself with a wry grin.

The atrium hadn't changed either. It was still a nice place to hang out. She could hear her mother, and took a final fortifying breath and walked toward the voices.

"Daddy," she said as they came into view.

Her father's grin made all the crap she knew was coming worth it. "Ariel," he said rising to his feet. "Porter didn't tell us you were here."

"I told him not to bother, I'd be right down." She hugged him, grateful to see how spry he appeared.

"Obviously," her mother said. "I see you didn't change."

Releasing her father, she faced her mother. As usual, the woman hadn't a single hair out of place. Her silk outfit, Ariel knew from experience, would have been expensive. She walked over and placed a kiss on her mother's cheek. "Good to see you as well, Mother."

The shoulder pat and air kiss were decidedly uncomfortable. "I expect you to dress for dinner."

"I've only eaten naked once but he asked me so nicely I couldn't find it in me to refuse."

Her mother's eyes widened. "Ariel, please. There is no reason to be crass."

"Do I need a reason other than it's fun?" She moved to the ottoman then sat and leaned back against the chair behind it. "Don't worry, Mother. I'll make sure to be *properly* attired for the evening meal."

"See that you do."

Ariel didn't even respond. Her mother loved having the last word and it made things in the house much simpler when she got her way. This woman would have had Hitler running to the Allies asking, begging to surrender if it would just get her off his back.

* * * *

The party was a hit. Trouble was, it lasted all day and by evening, Ariel wasn't in the best of moods. All this flash and pomposity wasn't her thing. She would have much rather taken her father to a steakhouse and had a beer with him. As she leaned against the marble balustrade, a shadow fell over her left shoulder.

Wishing it wasn't some trick played by the wine she'd had, she took a breath and looked. The man standing there was handsome. His three-piece suit had been tailored for him, she knew that from a single glance. There was no way ones off the rack draped that way.

She arched an eyebrow. "Can I help you?" *I bet this is what's-his-name that Mother wants me to mate with.*

He held out his hand, assuredness all over his behavior. "Dr Saunders. Aaron Saunders."

They shook and she smiled. "Ariel Greene."

His grin turned smug. "I know. Your mother showed me your picture."

"Did she now?"

"It didn't do you justice."

She retrieved her hand from his and drained the rest of her drink. Already her alarms were screaming to get away from him. "Mother says you're just a surgeon, not a specialist."

His expression sobered and he cleared his throat. "I'll be getting that soon."

She gave him a smile she'd seen her mother give many times. One that placated but wasn't at all impressed.

"She told me you would be interested in a date to see how well we get along."

"And then we can discuss marriage?"

"Yes. I mean I obviously like what I see and I know you do."

Oh, of all the unmitigated gall... Her fist clenched and she counted back from ten so she didn't punch him. All she did was smile and give a grunt of sorts.

"She says you love to cook. I think that's wonderful. I agree with your mother that women should be home, cooking for their children."

"Is that so? Did my mother tell you she never once cooked for us? Nor did she raise us. The servants and nanny did." She stepped closer. "I grew up loving beer and steak. Not wine. Although I do drink it occasionally. I also like my hard liquor. I swear like a sailor and I am not the docile type of woman my mother tries to pretend I am. If that's what you're after, you should probably talk with her about my other sister. She's a bit more primitive, like you and my mother."

He seemed taken aback. Ariel pressed on.

"I'm not a dainty housewife. I'm a Marine. I'm not supposed to tell you that because according to her, it's not ladylike. Well, I'm not very ladylike. I'm in this dress for my father. That's it. Not because you were coming and she hoped I'd fall madly in love with you. I'm already in love with someone and he does what my mother considers menial work. Good luck, *Doctor*. But you're not getting into this family through me." She shifted her weight. "If you'll excuse me, I am going to go pull this underwear out of the crack of my ass." She smirked. "It's just so uncomfortable some days."

Laughing, she walked away and went to her father's side. He was eating some of his cake but looked up when she approached.

"Time for you to go?"

"Sorry, Daddy, but I have to or I'm going to miss my flight."

He hugged her. "Don't stay away so long this time."

"I won't. You'll have to come down to San Antonio and we'll spend some time exploring."

His eyes brightened. "The Alamo?"

"Absolutely. I love you, Daddy."

He kissed her. "Love you too. Now go on before your mother finds another reason you can't possibly leave."

"Tell her goodbye for me."

He gave a sad smile. "Go."

She did, pausing to turn back when he called her name. "Yes, Daddy?"

"I'm proud of you, baby."

She blew him a kiss then headed for her car. Her bag had already been delivered there, thanks to Porter. And the man waited for her. Their farewell was similar to her father's. Then she was on her way back to the airport. She'd not even changed. Ariel had a singular destination in mind and nothing was going to keep her from arriving there as soon as she could. Nothing.

* * * *

The hushed voices sounded far away. Something that didn't make sense. Hushed meant they had to be close. Right?

He tried to open his eyes but it turned out to be such a battle. And took him more than one try. Soft light filled the room and he couldn't make any sense of where he was, based on the window view. Nothing rang familiar to him.

His nothing included the two men who stood talking at the end of his bed. *Well, I know where the voices came from.* Both tall, one in an expensive suit and the other had a stethoscope around his neck as well as a white lab coat.

Doctor. Still don't know who he is, though. Either of them. He continued glancing about the hospital room. Balloons touting "Get Well" were plentiful. As were plants, flowers and cards. *Guess people like me.*

Movement to his right had him peering there. *Damn!* A woman sat there. Sound asleep, sunk in the chair, with her head resting along the right corner of the back. Long hair framed the aristocratic lines of her face. Her dark skin shone and he had this inane urge to drag his fingers along it.

Who is she?

He closed his eyes, shifted on the bed then opened them again. The two men were hovering over him. The doc was talking—he didn't make sense of any of it, however—and the suit wearer had a wide grin.

Where is she?

Cutting his gaze to the right for a second time, he frowned when he didn't see her. He stared ahead and couldn't explain his relief when he saw her past the foot of the bed. She was awake now, and her brown gaze remained focused on him.

Some nurses came in and took him off the respirator, before rolling, poking, and even prodding him before they left him alone. He was exhausted.

Suit clutched his hand. "Damn good to see you awake, Pierce. I'll call your folks and they'll be right over. They're staying at a nearby hotel."

He racked his brain but couldn't pull up this man's name. His parents he remembered. And his siblings. *But why don't I know him? Or her?*

The suit stepped back and the woman took his place. She ran her gaze over him, eyes full of worry and relief. "Had us concerned there, Tuck. Glad you're awake." A soft yet sad smile. "I should call Steve — he'll want to hear you've woken up."

Steve? Not a brother. So who was that? Her husband? No, that didn't feel right. "Wait." His word was rough. She lifted her brow but didn't move. "Wh...who are you?"

"Don't worry about that."

Despite the words he could see the hurt in those stunning brown eyes. She reached out to touch him only to not allow the contact in the end. He was disappointed about that. Then she walked away.

His parents arrived and after the tears, hugs and more tears, he cleared his throat. "The man in the suit and the woman. Who are they?"

His mother's eyes grew wide and she grabbed at the doctor. "What's wrong with him?"

The doctor stood near and flashed a penlight in his eyes. "I would guess a form of retrograde amnesia. More recent activities are unable to be recalled. Remember, he's been in a coma for a good number of days. His body will undo what it did to protect him."

"Is it" — she lowered her tone — "permanent?"

"Time will tell. Most —"

"Oh my God!" she wailed.

The doctor held up his hand. "Most often it's short-lived and he will regain those memories."

His mother clasped her hand to her neck. "Thank you, Jesus."

When his father leaned close, he asked the question that had been bothering him since he saw her. "Who is she?"

"She was your neighbor, Ariel Greene. Friends with your roommate Steve."

Was his neighbor. Steve, the man Ariel had said she was going to call. He tested both names. Nothing. *Damn it!* "And the man?"

"Richard Dockett."

Recognition sparked. "He's in construction."

His father's face lit up. "And helped you start your company."

Okay, that didn't ring any bells. His company? He had a company? What the hell was happening there if he was in here?

"Don't worry, son. Richard is keeping an eye on everything for you."

He relaxed a bit. He may not remember him right out, but he did recall something about him. And he liked and trusted him. The doctor checked him again, asked some annoying questions then made notes on his chart before leaving.

"Dad?"

"Yes, son?"

"How are you affording to stay here?" His parents weren't wealthy.

"Mr Dockett put us up. Refused to even discuss payment. Just said parents shouldn't have to worry about money when their child is in the hospital."

Richard stepped back in the room, leaning heavily on his cane. He didn't speak but then, he didn't need to—he demanded attention just by walking in the door. He approached the bed as Tuck watched his parents embrace by the window.

"How are you doing, Pierce?"

"Feel like shit."

"Understandable."

"I'm told you put up my parents and took care of my work while I've been here. Thank you."

"Not a need to thank me, son. You focus on recovering. Your jobs are coming fine. Drake's stepped up big and is handling it all. Man's great with everything, it's like he's been doing it forever. You're going to love your house. It's just about done. Then they paint and lay carpet and you'll be able to move in."

Drake. His house. None of it was familiar and he shook his head. "Good to know," he managed to say with a smile.

"The w… Ariel, has she been here long?"

"Not immediately, but she was deployed to the Middle East. Once she came back, yes, she's been here pretty much all of her free time."

"Middle East?" Memories tingled. "She's a Marine."

"Yes."

So he knew some things but not others. His relationship with Ariel turned up nothing. Or about her. Other than she was a Marine. He glanced to the door, hoping she'd come back in. Something he continued to wish for even as he drifted off.

* * * *

Over the next few days many people visited. His memory hadn't healed and nurses told him Ariel sat with him as he slept. He realized he had to change his sleeping pattern.

It wasn't an easy thing for him to do but it worked and he woke to find her dozing in the corner chair. For a moment—okay, a few—he watched her. Everything in him was drawn to her.

He moved his fingers and angled the bed up higher. Her eyes were on him, sharp and alert. With a graceful motion, she rose and walked to his side before taking a seat.

"How are you feeling?"

"Sore." He gestured down his body. "Guess a shattered hip and leg will do that to a man."

"Reckon so."

"Tell me. Are we in a relationship?"

A wry smile as she fixed the pin on her shirt. It was familiar. The flames and the letters PP arranged in a shield.

"No."

That didn't seem right. "Are you sure?"

Her smile was wider now. "Quite. Would you like some water?"

He observed her as she poured him some then offered him the straw. The scent of lilacs surrounded him, bringing desire and comfort to him. Tuck—he preferred that name to Pierce—sipped and laid his head back once finished.

"Did we have a relationship?"

"For a time."

"And you broke up with me why?"

She retook her seat. He decided he favored her hair loose not drawn back as she wore it today.

"Why do you assume I broke up with you and not the other way around? Have you regained your memories?"

"No, I haven't. I assumed it went that way because while I can't recall much currently I'd like to think I'm not foolish enough to let you go."

She didn't seem impressed.

He shrugged. "You asked."

"Maybe I'm a cold-hearted bitch."

"You wouldn't be here if you were." That he was positive about.

She studied her nails. "Do you really think it productive to ask these questions?"

"Only if I want to learn what fool thing I was dumb enough to do which drove you away from me."

She was clearly uncomfortable. "There wasn't the respect I needed in a relationship."

He turned his head so he could see her without straining his eyes. "I didn't respect you?" More words that didn't ring right to him.

"It was a few things."

"Like?" He coughed. "No way I cheated."

Her expression gave him pause.

"Shit. I cheated? On you?" No way, he wasn't buying it.

"I don't know," she said softly.

There was more to it than that. "You thought I was."

She cracked her neck. "I had suspicions."

"If I did, I'm sorry. I know you probably don't care but it doesn't feel right in here"—he touched his heart—"that I would have done so."

She lifted a shoulder. "Like I said. I had no proof, only suspicion."

"And had you proof?"

"We wouldn't be having this conversation and you wouldn't be trying to remember me."

He held her gaze. "I *will* remember you."

"I'm sure you will." She checked her watch.

"Tell me about you."

"Me? What about me?"

"Anything. And us. Tell me about us. What we liked to do and all that." He winked. "I'm guessing there was a lot of sex."

She didn't comment, just narrowed her gaze a bit. He asked again for her to talk.

"Which do you want? About me or us?" She sipped from his glass, something he was happy to witness.

"All." He yawned. "I want to know it all."

She sat back and drummed her fingers along the chair's arm. "We met for the first time a bit over two years ago when I moved into the place across the hall from you and Steve."

He remembered that name. Not so much the man, but since he'd stopped by a few times, he did now. "My roommate."

"And friend, yes." Her fingers stilled. "We hit it off and would hang out together, share meals, things like that."

"We dated for that entire time?"

A short bark of laughter escaped her. "No. You..." She licked her lips and stared at the ceiling. "...led a very active social life."

"You're saying I slept with a lot of women."

Her grin came, a mysterious flash of white. "Maybe it was men."

He chuckled. *Feels good to do that.* "No way, babe. I was not wanting men. Not given how I'm trying to figure out how to make a pass at you now and see if I can convince you for a little hospital extra-curricular."

Another brief smile. "How do you intend to pull that off?"

"Give you puppy dog eyes and say it itches below the casts?"

"I could get you a clothes hanger."

"Your touch or nothing, babe."

"Sorry then. No extra-curricular will be happening."

"Damn. Fine then, tell me more."

"We hung out at baseball games, hockey and football. Most sports."

"Basketball?"

"You and Steve would go to Spurs games. They're your team."

"When did we date?" He moved his fingers. "How long?"

"Started in the summer and it ended on Thanksgiving."

Geez. What kind of ass was he that she ended it on a holiday? "Were we going to have a second go?"

"No."

He reached for her hand, first time he'd done so — to his personal recollection — and curved his fingers around hers. She watched him without any expression, which gave him a hint of what she was thinking.

"Can I change your mind?"

She squeezed his hand before disengaging them. "You have more important things to focus on than me." Ariel brushed some of his hair away from his face. "I have to get going. I'll see you."

He grabbed her again and pulled her close. They were nose to nose when he cupped the back of her head, fingers smoothing along her skin.

"Will you hurt me if I kiss you?"

"I might."

"Good thing I'm already in a hospital then."

He closed the distance and captured her mouth. She opened beneath his pressure and he sank his tongue into the heat he found. Flashes of memory hit him as if he were flicking through a camera's data. Images of him and her locked in erotic positions. His body reacted painfully and instantly. A groan slipped from him and she broke away.

"Goodbye, Tuck." She walked out.

It was only after she had left that he realized a nurse stood near, waiting. He looked at her.

"Yes?"

"Just time for your meds." She gave him a kind smile. "I figured they could wait for the kiss."

He was okay with that. As long as she didn't have to peer under the blanket— she was about the same age as his mother and he had no plans for letting her see his erection.

"She's a sweet one. And cute. Girlfriend?" She handed him the pills then topped off his glass of water Ariel had poured earlier.

"My future wife and mother of my children." He took his pills and reached for the drink she held out.

"Such an adorable couple." She waited until he'd swallowed them all before taking her leave.

Tuck leaned back and replayed the kiss in his head. Ariel smelled like lilacs and tasted like heaven. And yes, they were an adorable couple.

Chapter Sixteen

Ariel carried the two bags of groceries to her vehicle. A cold wind whipped around her and she merely wanted to get home and grab some sleep. Much needed sleep. Most of her free time had been spent at the hospital with Tuck.

He was remarkably upbeat given what had happened. He'd had pins placed in his hip and legs and was working on walking now. February had just begun and she was ready for April or so, when the weather was much nicer.

She put the bags in the back then closed the hatch. Fighting off a yawn, she got in behind the wheel. Today, she'd had a shitty day. Spending time with Tuck would have put her in a better mood but she didn't have time to visit. He was different and she understood it was because he was trying to recall the things he'd forgotten. It was very weird hanging out with him when she was the only one who knew what they'd gone through and done together.

Daily he asked her for specifics on reasons for their break-up. She didn't expound on it. If he didn't remember, there was no point in bringing it up.

"Let it go and get home, Ariel," she told herself as she stared at her reflection in the rear-view.

She drove to her new place. A small studio apartment. It wasn't bad but she hated having most of her things in storage. After arriving, she carried in her bags and had just finished putting her things away when her doorbell rang. A glance to the monitor and she smiled at the face she saw.

"Hey, Steve," she said opening the door.

"Hey, stranger. Got a minute?"

She waved him in. "Get you a drink?" Ariel closed the door.

"Please."

She popped open two beers and passed one along. "What's up?"

"Tuck comes home tomorrow."

"That's wonderful to hear."

He drank some beer. "It is."

"But?" she prompted.

"I have to leave for three days. I don't want him alone."

Her belly tightened. "What is it you want from me?"

"Stay with him. Keep an eye and stop him from trying to do too much."

"I don't know, Steve."

"You can stay in my room. He needs…us."

She toyed with her bottle. "So this would begin tomorrow?"

"Yes."

There wasn't a way for her to refuse. She couldn't. Not if she wanted to ever look at herself again without feeling shame. "Okay, I'm in. But I have to work in the morning."

"Thank you."

"Wanna stay for dinner?" She'd missed him and wanted to catch up.

Steve hugged her. "I hoped you'd ask. Smells delicious. What is it?"

"Slow cooker ribs."

"What can I do?"

"Salad stuff. Make yourself at home. I need a shower and change. Be right back." He toasted her with his beer.

Standing below the shower spray, she closed her eyes and braced her hands along the wall tiles.

Are you sure you're doing the right thing?

"Nope. Well, right thing? Yes. Smart? No."

Can you handle it?

"No choice, I have to." She began washing and tried not to think about Tuck. Or anything they'd done together.

Shower and dinner over, Ariel was horny as she headed to her room almost immediately after Steve had left. Naked, she crawled beneath her blankets and grabbed one of her vibrators. Turning it on, she ran it over her pussy, shuddering with a mix of anticipation and pleasure.

"Damn you, Tuck Carter."

She closed her eyes and focused on a mental memory of Tuck as she used *yet another* set of batteries to bring herself to orgasm.

* * * *

"How much did he pay you to stay here?" Tuck asked as he slowly made his way from his room to where she'd just put their dinner in the oven.

"Nothing."

"So then why?"

"Because Steve asked me." She smacked his hand when he reached for a beer. "None while on your meds. Water, tea, juice, or Coke." She rolled her eyes. "Or whatever kind he has in there."

"What?"

She was unmoved by his astonishment. "Steve gave me the list of alloweds and not alloweds."

"Bastard."

"I'm sure he's very hurt by your words."

"There's always tomorrow."

Ariel poured herself some tea then returned the pitcher to the fridge. "I'm working from here the next few days. Brought all I need to do that." His expression had her smirking, only it fell away when his gaze turned molten.

"So all day, it's just you and me?"

Heat flared in her belly and her clit throbbed. Ignoring those issues as well as her breasts growing heavy with want, she smiled. "Yes. Steve said you would be handling some things as well."

"And if I work naked?"

"Then you work naked." She turned to the fridge and pulled out some fruit.

"You know you're interested to see if I do."

She put the items down and arched an eyebrow. "Do it."

"Is that a challenge?"

Would he do that? "Take it as you will," she said.

"My scars won't offend you?"

Ariel didn't like the nervousness she picked up in his tone. "First, scars would never bother me, nor should they bother anyone worth a damn. Second, since I won't be looking at you, it's a moot point."

"Care to make a wager on that, babe?"

She faced him and arched a brow. "What's the bet?"

"When you lose" — he raked his gaze over her — "you give me the truth on what broke us up."

"And when I win?"

"Not happening. And I'm so confident, you can have whatever you want."

Oh, the temptation. She held out her hand. "Deal. You're going to owe me big."

"We'll see," he said with a decadent chuckle. "We will see about that."

"Yes we shall." She turned away from him and focused on fixing the fruit salad. These three days would not be boring, that was already obvious.

* * * *

Tuck rubbed his hip, scowling at the scars beneath his fingertips. He could hear Ariel as she fixed breakfast. This was her last day here. It sucked that he couldn't remember what it was he'd done to her. All he knew was that she was making this recovery so much better. Bearable. Doable.

Beneath his blankets, his cock twitched and stiffened. He wanted her. Craved the feel of her pussy gripping his shaft. Heat curled around him. He knew they'd been together, for he continually had images of them, naked limbs entwined. Faces contorted in the throes of passion. But he couldn't *remember* how it felt to make love to her. A fact he couldn't bear.

It had to have been amazing.

He slid a hand down to his insistently throbbing cock. Up and down, he began to stroke himself. Head back and eyes closed, he ran his hand along the length, stimulating the head and his balls.

What was her touch like? He moved faster. *Softer? No, she has a strong grip.*

Dredging up the scent of lilacs, he tightened his hold as he fisted himself faster until he came with a low shout. Thick ropes of his cum ran over his hand.

"Tuck?" she asked from the door. "Are you okay?"

"Fine," he gritted out. "Just stepped wrong. I'll be out soon."

"Okay."

"Way to go, asshole," he muttered as he carefully made his way from the bed to his bathroom. "Get her in here as you jack off because you can't keep quiet about coming."

After he'd cleaned himself up, he picked up his pants only to pause. "Going to work naked, today."

The first night, she'd set up a desk for him in the living room so he didn't have to spend the day sequestered in his room. At his urging, she'd set one up for herself as well. This way he'd be able to see her watching him as they'd faced one another. She'd given him a knowing smirk each day he'd come out with pants. But that wouldn't be happening today.

He knew Ariel didn't think he would do it but he had no intention of losing this bet. Opening his door, he carefully made his way to the kitchen. The scent of waffles permeated the air. Smelled good. Ariel smelled better, however.

Her pair of heather-gray workout pants rode low on her hips and she had a black Missions jersey on.

"Morning," he said.

"Morning," she replied without turning around.

"Smells great." He went to the fridge then opened the door, knowing she would be made aware of his naked state then.

"Th...thanks."

He smirked. That stutter was for him. After grabbing the juice, he closed the door — it was cold in there with nothing protecting the family jewels. Her gaze was firmly affixed to the plate of bacon she had at her elbow.

"Something wrong?" he asked, standing beside her, making sure to brush against her.

"Nope." Her voice came out much higher than it usually was.

"Not going to look at me?"

Her eyes met his after a pregnant pause, her expression now composed. "Sorry, fixing breakfast. Was there something specific you wanted me to see?"

He shrugged. "Just wanted to see those eyes of yours."

"Good for you." She turned her head away. "Breakfast is ready. Grab a seat."

"Awesome. I'm starved."

Her mutter wasn't anything he could understand. He took his seat and sucked a deep breath at how cold it was. Ariel hadn't turned around. He stared at her back and watched as she took several deep breaths.

Good, he was getting to her.

She carried both plates over and handed him his before going back for his drink. His unruly cock decided to misbehave during the meal. Ariel kept her gaze on the wall across from her. She didn't say much but he didn't push it. He was trying not to get syrup all over his dick.

"I have to start working," she announced, standing. More of those deep breaths as she stood in the kitchen facing the sink.

He finished off his last bite and got up to stand behind her. Reaching around her, he placed his plate in the sink. He slid some of her hair to the side and kissed her neck. "Thank you."

Tuck went to his work station and sat, only to get up and put down a towel. He needed something between his ass and the chair. Sneaking a glance to Ariel, he found her focused on her computer screen, face scrunched.

"You okay?" he asked.

She blinked and looked at him. Just his face, her eyes didn't go any lower than that. "Sure, why?"

"You looked confused there. Or upset."

"I'm fine. You?"

"A bit of a headache." That was the truth.

"Do you want some pills?"

"Not right now. Thanks, though."

The morning passed with him not getting much done at all. Damn if she wasn't good about not looking at him. He, on the other hand, couldn't seem to keep his eyes off her and was getting shit done.

He picked up his head and focused on her again. She'd captured her lower lip in her teeth as her fingers flew along the keyboard of her laptop. This wasn't fair — he was supposed to be the distraction.

A knock on the door had them both pausing. She met his gaze briefly before turning back to where the sound had originated.

"Who is it?" he called out.

"Drake."

Ariel laughed.

"Just a minute, Drake." He pointed at her. "What's so funny?"

"Planning on entertaining in your birthday suit?"

"Shit!"

She stood up. "I'll let him in."

"Ariel, come on. Help me out here."

"Thought you wanted to work naked?"

"Woman," he rumbled.

She laughed harder. "Would you like a shirt? Maybe they can't see under the desk."

"You're evil."

Ariel walked out of the room then returned moments later with a pair of his sweats and a shirt. "Come on, up you get."

He stood. "Already up, babe. Been that way since breakfast. But I know you know, since I've caught you looking."

She wove a bit, coming closer before she regained control. He gasped when her hand curved around his shaft. Not that her breathing was any better. Her thumb skimmed the head of his cock, smearing the drop of pre-cum that had leaked the second she touched him.

"You're bad for me," she murmured, releasing him before she went to her knees. "So bad." Her breath was warm along his shaft.

"Ariel."

"Balance on my shoulder and put your feet in the pants."

He did as she ordered and wanted to weep in sexual frustration as she stood up and backed away.

"Shirt on." He sat and drew it on over his head.

She opened the door and stepped back.

"Hey, Ariel."

"Drake. Sorry, I had to come from the other room."

She lied so smoothly. Drake's gaze moved around the apartment almost like he expected to see proof of their illicit rendezvous.

"Come on in." Ariel went back to her desk and sat.

Behind Drake came a redhead. She smiled at him and he flashed a quick peek to Ariel. She was just taking her gaze from the woman. Her entire expression was closed off.

But Tuck knew who she was. He knew.

"Hi, Daisy," he said. "What's up, Drake?"

Ariel beheld him for a short time before going back to the stuff she had to do. Drake and Daisy approached him and caught him up to speed on the jobs at hand.

"Thanks for taking such good care of everything, Drake."

"Not a problem, man. Well, I'd better get going. The house looks great. The colors you picked work wonderfully."

He couldn't wait to see it himself. "Thanks. Is the stuff for the party set up?"

"I have that information here," Daisy said, stepping closer.

Tuck snuck another look at Ariel. Everything was clear now, he had it all back. Including why she'd broken it off with him.

Chapter Seventeen

Ariel swore as she pumped the weights. The torment within her hadn't given her a moment's rest. And she hated every second of it.

"Hey, you got a moment?" Slater popped out of nowhere to sit beside her on the next machine.

"I'm working out, where am I going to go?"

"Can you listen?"

"Rumor has it I do."

"Are you going tonight?"

"No." She didn't even make him wait to elaborate on what he was asking about. She knew already. They'd been discussing it since the invites had arrived.

"Are you sure?"

"Spending my night at the opening party of Carter Architectural and Construction is not on my to-do list."

Slater shook his head. "You know he invited you."

"I've already congratulated him on his success."

"Are you positive you're not going to go?"

She paused on the lat machine and glared at him. "Want me to spell it out for you? I'm not going."

"Okay, okay. I just wanted to make sure because there's a meeting I'm going to send you to instead to meet a potential client."

She began drawing down on the bar again. "Seriously, Slater? Tonight?"

"Hey, I asked you first if you were going to this other thing. You said you weren't. So I need you to do this instead."

She stopped and reached for her towel, wiping her face. "Fine. What's the address?"

He handed her the slip of paper. She read it and didn't recognize it at all.

"What time?"

"He said eight."

"Very well. I'll do it."

"Thanks, Ariel." He smiled and got to his feet. "Appreciate it."

"Right," she muttered, getting back to her workout, leaving the address by her water bottle on the floor.

She ran like crazy all day long and was surprised at five when Connie popped her head in the door.

"We're going to the party. Wish you were coming with me."

"Please. You have Slater. I'm sure whatever dirty act you two come up with doing in some closet I'm not going to be needed for."

The woman waggled her eyebrows.

"Should I have bail money ready?"

"I think so." Connie waved. "See you tomorrow."

"Have fun."

Her phone rang at six and she answered. "Hello?"

"Couldn't even come to my party?"

"Didn't think it would be needed."

"You were my friend, Ariel. Are, you are my friend."

She tapped her nails on the desktop. "I still am but I couldn't get away from work. Besides, I've already congratulated you on your business."

"I remember that night," he said, voice low and tempting. "I took you over the table. Your panties were around your ankles and your skirt bunched up at your waist. Do you remember? How wet you were? The feel of my cock as it slammed into you, making the table shake and groan. Over and over you orgasmed, coating me with your thick cream."

She trembled as he painted his picture. "I... I have to go. Congrats again, Tuck."

"Ariel, wait."

"I can't. I have another client to meet tonight and have to get going." She hung up before he could say anything else. She sat at her desk, her harsh breaths filling the air until she got herself back under control.

"Damn him," she cursed. "God damn him."

She threw herself back into her work, wrapping it all up when her alarm went off. She had a distance to go and didn't want to be late. She made sure to grab a coffee along the way and turned on the radio.

The song by Jake Owen, *Alone With You*, came on and she blinked away tears as the meaning of the words sank in. It was like her and Tuck's relationship. She'd been drunk the first two times they'd been together.

He made her crazy and it was hell being alone with him, for all she thought about was making them both insane with lust. If he was a drug, he was her choice to take. She needed to find a way to get past this before she drove herself bonkers.

She got nearer to her destination and overlooked the house as she made her way up the driveway. Dirt road. A two-story house with a lovely front porch.

Very nice. In the drive near the house was a white Cadillac Escalade. She parked beside it and got out.

The stars shone above her and she took a minute to enjoy them. The sounds of the city were non-existent here and she took a deep breath, pleased to not be sucking down exhaust fumes or worse.

With a sigh, she jogged up the steps then rang the doorbell. Readjusting her folder beneath her arm, she waited for the door to open. When it did she nearly dropped all her papers.

Tuck.

She drew back, recovering quickly, and stared at the house number. She was at the right place.

"What are you doing here?" she asked.

"Won't you come in?"

"Damn it, what the hell are you doing here?"

His gaze ran over her face. "It's my house. Come in and we can talk inside."

"You…your house?"

"Christ, Ariel. Get in here." He reached for her but she sidestepped him and entered the foyer. "Was that so difficult?"

That remains to be seen. Oh, God help me. I'm alone in a house with him in the middle of nowhere. Then again, perhaps I'm not alone.

"Why the subterfuge?" she demanded, trying not to look at the beautiful work done in the entrance.

"Because you refused to take any more of my calls. Or return any messages." He crossed his arms and stared down at her. "That, and I want a security system put in here."

"So call ADT. There's nothing left for us to say to one another."

"Bullshit."

"I don't have time to be jerked around."

"You set time for this appointment. Give me that time, Ariel. If what I have to say doesn't sway you, I promise I'll leave you alone."

"For how long?"

He held her gaze. "Forever. Give me a chance to explain."

She shifted her folder from one side to the other. "Are you serious about having a system?"

"Absolutely. And if you don't want to deal with me after this, I'll tell Slater to send someone else."

"Let's do that first. Then I'll listen."

"Your word?"

She licked her lips. "You have it."

A tentative smile lifted his bow-shaped lips. "Thank you."

She trailed along behind him as he walked through his house, making notes as she would with any other client. The walls were done in neutral colors and tasteful art filled it. When he stopped outside his bedroom, he paused.

"What's wrong?" she asked, totally in work mode.

"I didn't want you to feel uncomfortable."

"I've been in your bedroom before, Tuck. Is there a woman in there?"

"Really, Ariel? You think I would ask you to give me a chance to explain and have a woman in my bedroom waiting for you to find her?"

"Nope." She watched him with her brow raised.

"So then what..." he trailed off. "Oh, I get it." He swung open the door.

Where the rest of the house may have been neutral, this room was vibrant. The rich blue thrummed through her blood as did the splashes of red. She couldn't help but be drawn to the large bed. However, it was what was across from it that stopped her in her tracks.

He had a wall like in the restaurant they'd gone to on their first date. As with the one there, his had colors behind it that slowly melded from one to the next. It calmed the room down but didn't kill it.

"Oh my God," she whispered. This is incredible. You get to lie in bed and watch that?"

"Well, took some getting used to so that I didn't have to get up and pee every hour but I'm attached to it now."

She gave a soft laugh. "This is a beautiful house, Tuck."

"You really like it?"

"It's gorgeous."

"Good," he said.

"Okay, I've gotten what I need. So, I owe you some time. Where are we going to do this?"

His gaze flashed to the bed and she grunted. He beckoned and she went to his side and peered up at him.

"Bed's not happening."

"Night's still young, babe. I was thinking the den, though."

She locked her body's traitorous behavior in a box and followed his fine ass down the stairs to his kitchen, where he made her a hot cocoa with marshmallows and a coffee for himself then led the way to his den.

"Where are you sitting?" he asked.

"Why?"

"So I can sit opposite you and see your eyes."

His words warmed her in ways the hot cocoa never could. She took the love seat and put her folder beside her. Tuck did as he'd said, taking the tall leather chair across from her. He moved so much better now but she could still see some stiffness in him.

The light from the fire to his right added a bit of mystery to him. Didn't take anything away from how good he looked, though, and she knew he would always be important to her.

So why have you been avoiding him?

Stupid brain. Not a question she cared to answer.

"I love you," he said.

She nearly dropped her drink. It wobbled and almost sloshed over the side as it was. "Wh...what did you say?"

"You heard me, Ariel. I said I love you. I've loved you almost since we met. I can't say it was love immediately but damn near. I'm saying this now, before I explain anything else because if you run out before I'm done, this way you'll still know how I feel. I won't have missed another opportunity to tell you how much I love you."

Damn, she wanted to cry.

Tuck watched her face. He knew she was shocked. She had the look of an animal who was currently deciding between fight and flight. He didn't move, waiting for her to make up her mind. If she ran now, he would honor his promise to her and leave her alone. He didn't want to but he would.

"Why would you just blurt something like that out?" she asked, placing her mug beside her on the end table. She picked it up again and slid a coaster beneath it.

"Because I wanted you to know."

It wasn't easy staying in his chair but he forced himself to do so.

Once he was sure she had committed to staying, he sipped some coffee and leaned forward, resting his arms on his quads.

"I know I made a mistake with the whole Daisy issue. Part of me knew I should tell you but part didn't want a fight to come from it, so I ignored it. Basically convincing myself you'd never find out. She was with a temp agency, I didn't think she'd be around long."

Her eyes narrowed.

"She turned out to be a whizz at this job and I made it permanent. I know, I know. It was stupid and foolish, for which I'm sorry. But believe me, I never slept with her after that first time when you showed up in the apartment. Hell, I've not been with any other woman since you and I first had sex."

"Really?"

"I swear. I've only wanted you, Ariel. Since we met. No one else makes my heart race. No one else makes me smile or laugh as you do. No one else makes me feel like a man who can take on anything. You do. Always have."

"Don't be crazy. You don't need me."

"That's where you're wrong. I do need you. I need you in my life. I want to marry you. Have babies with you." A grin. "Well, you'll do the actual having, I just get to get you pregnant."

She shrank back against the love seat, eyes wide. Was it too much to hope there were tears there?

"I want to raise our children with you and grow old with you at my side. All this" — he waved his hand around — "I built with you in mind, Ariel. All of it."

"You don't like my job or some of the men I work with."

"No man wants to know his woman is in danger. But your job, both of them, is part of what makes you

you, Ariel. And I can't love you without accepting that."

She wrapped her arms around herself and drew her feet up to rest on the cushion. Tuck wondered if he'd gone too fast. Said too much too soon. She worried her lower lip and he left his seat to crouch before her. The pain in his hip had him flinching but he ignored it.

"You shouldn't be down there. What about your injuries?"

"I don't care."

"Well, I do. Get up." He didn't move. "Get up, Tuck."

"Will you stay there if I sit beside you?"

"Yes, just stop doing that."

He sat on the cushion and immediately felt better. "Come here." He pulled her close. "Can you give us another chance?" He kissed the top of her head. "Will you?"

She didn't answer and he wondered if he'd fucked up too many times for her to let it go.

"You know the first time I saw her in your truck I wanted to hit you. Then it happened a few more times. I waited for you to say something to me about her working with you. That's the respect I need. I don't ever want you to feel like you need to clear an employee with me for your business. But if it's a woman you've shared fluids with, I'd like a bit of a heads-up."

"Does that mean you're going to give us a chance?"

"I came to a realization when I got the note from Slater about your accident." She fell silent.

"What was that?"

"That I was still in love with you, despite having broken up on Thanksgiving."

His heart jumped for joy but then he registered the totality of her words. "Wait a minute, you still loved me? When did you fall in love with me?"

"A while ago."

"And you never told me?"

"You didn't say anything to me either."

She had a valid point there.

"I said it first now, though."

"Humph."

"Stay." He spoke into her hair. "Move in."

"Isn't that kind of fast?"

"The way I see it, we've been in love for two years. Why wait longer?"

She rubbed her cheek against his chest. "Why the rush?"

"Because I want to practice getting you pregnant."

She smacked him in the arm.

"I want you to wear my ring. Carry my name."

"What about Steve?"

He frowned. "The man has his own wife. He's not sharing mine."

"I meant will he be okay if you move out?"

"I've been packing for a while now. He's about to head back to his wife and see if he can't get her back anyway."

"So you want me to move in here and what…? Live in sin?"

"I'll marry you anytime, babe. But we can live that way if you want."

She released a deep breath.

"What's wrong, Ariel? Worried about your family?"

"I am now."

"You told me about them and I'm capable of holding my own."

"No one holds their own with my mother."

"I have a mother too, you know."

"Not like mine."

"Good, then I can charm her."

Her laugh was strained. Readjusting her so he could see her face, he put his finger under her chin.

"No family to think about. Nothing but you and me. Are you in, Ariel?"

She studied his face for a while then swallowed her remaining fear. "Absolutely."

"I love you."

She wrapped her arms around his neck. "I love you, too, Tuck."

"You're calling in to work tomorrow. I want you for the next few days to myself." He kissed her with all the love and passion he had in him. "I want to be alone with you."

"Sounds perfect to me," she whispered as she guided their lips back together.

About the Author

Aliyah Burke is an avid reader and is never far from pen and paper (or the computer). She is married to a career military man, and they have a German Shepherd, two Borzois, and a DSH cat. Her days are spent sharing her time between work, writing, and dog training.

Aliyah Burke loves to hear from readers. You can find her contact information, website details and author profile page at http://www.totallybound.com.

Totally Bound Publishing